Route 66 Sweetheart

by Michael Lund

BeachHouse Books

Chesterfield Missouri USA

Copyright

The poems attributed in this story to Ethel Woodruff Lacy are, in fact, compositions of the author's maternal grandmother, Ethel Woodruff Macy. Some were published in literary magazines during her lifetime, and her work was featured in Michael Lund and Robert W. Hamblin's *"About a Little Girl": A William Carlos Williams Poem and its Legacy* (Southeast Missouri State University Press, 2008).

Graphics Credits:

Cover design and graphics by John Lund.

Publication date 2011

ISBN 9781596300705 BeachHouse Books Edition

Library of Congress Cataloging-in-Publication Data

Lund, Michael, 1945-
  Route 66 sweetheart / by Michael Lund. -- Beachhouse books ed.
      p. cm.
  ISBN 978-1-59630-070-5 (alk. paper)
1. United States Highway 66--Fiction. 2. Reminiscing in old age--Fiction.
3. Depressions--1929--Fiction. I. Title.
  PS3562.U486R6835 2011
  813'.54--dc22

                            2011019627

www.beachhousebooks.com

an Imprint of

Science & Humanities Press

PO Box 7151

Chesterfield, MO 63006-7151

(636) 394-4950

www.beachhousebooks.com

At Home and Away

by Michael Lund

This five-volume novel series chronicles an American family during times of peace and war from 1915 to 2015. The first book, *Route 66 Sweetheart*, is set mostly in and around Rutherford, New Jersey, during the 1930s, where a young woman who traces her ancestry back to the early New World settlement of Nantucket comes to maturity during the Depression. The second will feature the Missouri-born son of a Swedish immigrant who, in the early 1940s, pursues his dreams of American success in a land haunted by the prospect of approaching war. However, in both books some family members move away to distant countries and unexpected challenges.

Volume Three will take place primarily in the Midwest during the 1950s and '60s, but characters in that book also travel far from home and the comforts of a familiar world. The fourth volume follows another generation of family members, this time from Missouri to Southeast Asia and back again. In the final installment of the saga, their children travel from Virginia and North Carolina through Europe and the Middle East to understand their identity in a multi-national community.

Acknowledgements

Authors routinely thank their publishers--we're so happy to get into print! My gratitude to Dr. Bud Banis goes deeper than that, though I, too, admit to pleasure at this book's appearance. I have felt a part of BeachHouse Books' larger enterprise from the moment I received a first letter of encouragement in 1999. And while I pray that the operation is always in the black, the true rewards of our joint efforts have come from the work itself--the writing, editing, printing, and distribution of books we value. In an industry undergoing radical revolutions in production, BeachHouse has remained true to the finest traditions of book making.

I owe Jim Shifflett thanks one more time for reading an early version of this manuscript and acknowledge that his insights have significantly improved the final product. I am also deeply grateful for his professional editing of the penultimate version. John Lund composed the cover, choosing, on his own, colors that match the tastes of the woman who inspired the central character and a design that enriches and extends the goals I had in writing this book. Thank you, John.

As always, any errors in fact or inconsistencies of narration in the pages that follow are attributable solely to the author.

For Marian Woodruff Macy Lund
and Ethel Woodruff Macy

Prologue: Who Comes First?

We're not the famous Lacys, the ones who founded a department store dynasty generations ago. That family who regularly receive honorary degrees from prestigious universities? Not us. Nor can we claim relatives who will sit on powerful corporate and charitable boards as far into the future as you can predict. But my Lacys trace our ancestors back to the same Thomas they do, one of nine men who bought Nantucket Island in 1659 for some cash and two beaver hats, launching the first English settlement in Massachusetts.

My children say I'm the matriarch of this less famous Lacy clan, and they're planning a grand reunion of the extended family to coincide with my 100th birthday party on July 4, 2015. Good for them. I tell them I'm just a 66 sweetheart, not the base of any family tree.

Still, anticipating my 100th, I have decided to begin telling our Lacy story to my son, a recently retired English professor. He's skeptical that I can do it at my age. But at his age (merely 65), he doesn't understand the strength of will that drives us as we see life's end approaching.

I said to him when I turned ninety-five last week-- they made a big deal of that birthday, but wait until they learn what I have in store for their reunion!--I said, "Curtis, I want you to do something for me."

"Of course, Nana." That's what I've been called since my first child was born, seldom the "Mid" I was as a girl or the "Marian" you'll find on my birth certificate and wedding license.

"Can I get you more cake? Are you ready for a rest? I can walk with you to your room."

For such a smart man, Curtis sometimes loses track of the big picture. "I want you to listen to me."

"I'm listening." He wasn't really, his head cocked toward what was going on outside.

"I want you to listen to me for thirty minutes each week for the next five years."

That caused him to look back at me. "I come by to visit that often nearly every day. Now that I'm retired, I could be here even more. And, of course, you'll live until you're 100."

I could see him glancing over my shoulder into the yard where his grandchildren were playing bocce. He really wanted to be out there with Beth, his wife. In many ways, so did I.

"Listening is just the first part. Then I need you to write it down, put it in proper form. You know, the way you do when you write about those Victorian authors you like so much."

"Dickens, and Eliot, Elizabeth Gaskell and Thomas Hardy. Yes, I suppose I could do that. But they wrote long stories, Nana. As serials in monthly magazines, their tales often ran for a year and a half, even two years in some cases."

There was a chorus of cheering outside. Someone's team must have won a round. They were playing on the back lawn that stretches down to a bulkhead in the idyllic village he and Beth had

2

discovered a decade ago. On weekends and in the summers, they've been restoring the two-story frame house they bought from the family of an old friend, readying it for occasions like this one. I recently moved to a retirement village fifteen miles away.

"My story is going to take five years to read, not eighteen months," I told him, with a smile of satisfaction. This idea had taken final shape only during the last week, with so many of my children and grandchildren gathered around me. "Let me ask you something: do you remember what you told me once about your ninth grade history class?"

"When I was thirteen? That's half a century ago!"

"That's when it happened, but you told me about it . . . I don't recall . . . perhaps five years ago. The class was discussing twin princes, one of whom would become the next king."

"Oh, now I remember. Because they were twins, no one could say who was older, and therefore who had the right to the throne."

"Correct. It must have been in some history class, about ninth grade."

Now it's coming back, what I blurted out." He laughed. "And then wished I hadn't."

There was another round of squealing from the yard, and Beth bustled through the door smiling. An island counter separated the family room (where we were) from the kitchen (where she was). And we could see her preparing for dessert--pie and ice cream. As we numbered at least thirty-five now that the West Coast children were here, she would need a hand.

"Curtis, help your wife. We'll finish this conversation when everyone is served. I'm going to move to the screen porch for a few minutes."

The L-shaped porch off the kitchen was half the size it had been when the house was built. A leg had been enclosed to create the present kitchen, turning the original kitchen into a large family room. Both spaces had bow windows opening out to the water. Later today the setting sun would throw its horizontal rays across tidewater North Carolina to illuminate houses on the opposite shore of the Perquimans River. It's always a glorious sight I can enjoy from the room I stay in, as well as from where I settled on the porch swing.

This water reminds me of my childhood, summers on Greenwood Lake in northern New Jersey. There, sunrise was spectacular, especially on crisp spring mornings. Now that I think about it, my life has been bracketed by water. Most of my middle years were spent in the heart of the country, a small Missouri town on Route 66; but water defines my beginning and end.

"Pie without ice cream, right?" said John, perhaps my favorite (male) grandchild.

"Of course. When it's a good pie, we don't add toppings." He smiled and patted my shoulder. Nice boy!

His dad joined me with his pie á la mode, and I resumed my tale.

"You said the obvious back when you were in ninth grade, what everyone was thinking about kings and princes, inheritance and family lines. But the others were afraid to say it. Of course, in those days one never mentioned the details of childbirth. That was forbidden talk, especially at school."

"Well, we've come a long way since then! As your grandchildren are learning, there's very little young people can't or won't discuss!"

"Well, you're referring to what they understand about sex, of course, because of the twins question. But there are new codes of silence now. Try to talk about how the same people who sit at the heads of U.S. corporations are also officers in international trade organizations, how former bankers become government regulators of the financial industry, how media conglomerates have friends where copyrights and patents are given. Don't tell me public discourse doesn't have its gaps!"

"Nana, you've become such a radical! But I know what you mean. Language always has its silences. But back then, I couldn't believe I'd blurted out such a shameful thing."

"As I remember, the class had all sorts of ideas about which twin should be king: the taller, the faster, the stronger. And one argued it should be the one with the louder voice."

"That was Larry, who became a lawyer and then a judge, a man who can talk."

"But you gave the right answer for an aristocratic social structure: 'the one who came out first.'"

"Oh, but what a terrifying answer that was! It brought into the minds of young children the image of a mother's womb, the act of birth! We were never supposed to picture that."

"Oh, the horrors of a baby emerging from such a place!"

"You should have seen the teacher's face! We moved on to Henry VIII and his many wives so quickly that the other question was forgotten. But why are you remembering that experience, an educational one, to be sure?"

"First, because for years I thought I was myself neither first nor last, only some meaningless point between the two. But also, there are other matters we've hidden over my lifetime, gaps I intend to fill in with the Lacy story. I want to talk about me, my siblings, my children and grandchildren.

"You're going to make us look at things we've been afraid to see?"

"Afraid, yes. But just as with your class debate, sometimes without reason. After all, somewhere in the 1960s we figured out--well, women figured out--there was nothing wrong with watching a child being born. In fact, it's a sight we should celebrate, not keep hidden."

You have a point. In earlier centuries, people--well, men really, who shaped language then--referred to it as a woman's 'confinement.' Those frightening creatures and what they do had to be contained, walled in."

"Well, I hope you're willing to open some doors with me. I'm going to tell you what I've learned about war in nearly a century, one part at a time, in installments."

"About war? Well, that's a big enough subject to make up a whole book."

I took my last bite of pie. "It will be about peace as well as war. We'll do one volume every year, five in all. This is the first chapter of book one. Write it down."

Volume One: Indoors and Out.
Chapter One: Here I Am!

To Marian, growing up in northeastern New Jersey just across the Hudson River from New York City, the important things in life seemed either very far away or almost too close. What mattered was out of reach or suffocating. She could find little middle ground.

Marian's father had not been sent "over there" during World War I because she and her two older siblings, John and Ella, had been born by 1917. But Curtis was profoundly affected by that historic conflict. And he was away from home frequently during the years his children were growing up (in addition to Marian, there would be two more, Alice and Bill).

Curtis Lacy rode the train to work in Manhattan every weekday. And, as a marine insurance adjustor, he often traveled to coastal and river cities throughout the country. A few times he went overseas for months at a time. So, one of the most consistent images of Marian's childhood was the figure of her father disappearing down Ridge Road as he strode briskly toward the train station in early morning light. Away.

Mid's two sisters and two brothers, on the other hand, were so close at home they often seemed to stifle her. Not that she didn't love them (and the two grandparents who had lived with them in their

9

widowhood), but if she'd had her own room (rather than sharing with Ella and Alice), or if she'd had some secret hideout like Judy Bolton in her favorite children's stories, she felt she could have maintained a better balance in her day-to-day affairs.

Her mother seldom left the house or its flower garden, but she often seemed distant. Marian assumed this was because Mrs. Ethel Lacy was thinking of grown-up things children would not understand. What her mother was contemplating would become clear only years later, however, at the time of her father's unexpected death.

The middle Lacy child also couldn't know for more than a decade that the man who would become the father of her children was half a continent away, moving with his carpenter father and school teacher mother from job to job in a Midwest hard hit by the Depression. They would not live in the same city until well after she became a 66 Sweetheart.

Marian's sense that she had either to get away from a crowded house or find a retreat deeper within it was made most distinct one summer day in the 1930s. Her older brother, John, was a student at M.I.T, coming home only on occasional weekends. The next in age, Ella, considered the family beauty, was being courted by high school classmates and a few college men, so the three younger siblings often played together in the evenings.

While Marian, Alice, and Bill were having a three-handed cribbage tournament, their mother was sitting on the sofa organizing family pictures into a new album.

"Mother?" Mid asked. "What's that?" The question was, she thought, rhetorical. Every time her mother arranged photos, the topic of Ethel's lost brother surfaced. And she would tear up.

"It's Uncle Henry, isn't it?" Alice whispered to Marian.

"Muggins!" exclaimed Bill. Alice had failed to count his nobs, but it wasn't clear that she'd finished totaling her score.

Marian intervened, putting a hand on Bill's shoulder and pulling him toward her. "That's not fair; we were talking to Mother. Mother, what is that picture?"

Ethel did have her characteristic faraway look, and her eyes were moist. Marian assumed she was thinking of Henry, their uncle who had disappeared more than a dozen years earlier. A bachelor at thirty-five, he'd gone on a business trip to Canada and never returned. There were stories in the papers of a train wreck outside Toronto, and the family came to believe he must have been aboard. But the fact that nothing could be confirmed inspired a number of stories.

"No, Alice. It's not my brother." Like most mothers, she could somehow understand her children's whispering. "It's about Mid," she explained.

"Me? Let me see." All three climbed up from the rug, Bill trying to push past Alice.

"That's not a picture," he noted.

"It's a poem, a poem about your sister."

"Let us read it!" commanded Alice.

But Ethel tucked the folded paper back into the album. "Let me tell you about it instead." She pulled Bill close. The sisters settled themselves on two wingback chairs. "You were too young to remember, but one summer Marian got very, very sick."

"That time I had the flu?"

"Yes. At least, that's what we thought it was. Then Dr. Paterson did this test--a blood test of some kind, I think. Two days later he gave us bad news: leukemia. "

Alice gasped. "You die from that!"

"Yes, you do. There was no treatment for it then, and there's none now either."

"The test must have been wrong," said Bill. "Here she is!"

"Here I am, yes," mused Marian. This year in biology class she had been introduced to a microscope. She would use many more in her ten-year career as a medical technologist, finding and drawing such tiny creatures that--though less than a foot from her careful eye--they seemed to exist in another, faraway universe. She imagined Dr. Paterson studying her blood, finding oddly shaped cells, a sign of destiny.

"I remember that summer. We were getting ready to go to the lake when I got so sick I couldn't get out of bed."

The family had a campsite on Greenwood Lake where they stayed from early summer until school began again in the fall, though Curtis had to commute into the city every weekday.

"Not so many had flu that year, not like it had been in 1918 or '19, but you were just as ill."

"I remember the war was over, though there were ever so many wounded and sick soldiers. Anyway, I do know that Doctor Paterson said I had to rest. I went to bed, and you put away all our camping equipment."

"It was weeks before you were well. We were never sure what your condition was, though it couldn't have been leukemia. And we even went to the lake after all. We got there just in time for Fourth of July. What a celebration! Fireworks over the water, and . . . "

"And?"

"Well, Dr. Paterson came to visit our campsite. It was just two tents back then. But the doctor brought me a present. Or perhaps it was for Father. They were fast friends."

"A keepsake?"

"You could say that--the poem." She patted the album. "He wrote a lot of poems. They tell me he's become pretty well known, especially in Europe. But I never could understand them. The things he wrote were just . . . sort of like snapshots, a picture of some scene."

"Was the poem about Mid, then?" asked Alice.

"It told about the whole family, our going to the lake. In the poem a little child is sick, and then she seems to die and rise up as some kind of angel."

13

"She doesn't act like an angel now," argued Bill.

Their mother laughed. "No, but neither do you, young man. Now, back to your game. I've got things to do in the kitchen." She rose, taking the album with her.

Sensing finality in this statement, Marian herded her younger siblings back to the rug, and the game resumed. But as she played, she tried to imagine the poem's words. She pictured herself as the child in the poem, an indistinct figure kept at a distance for some reason by her mother. It was a shadowy figure, a ghost of a girl perhaps.

When she'd been sick, she'd drifted in and out of dreams, rising and falling from restless sleep. The real world had seemed far away then--her older brother and sister at play in another room, neighbors strolling past on a Sunday afternoon, distant trains rolling north and south. She didn't know where she was or where she was supposed to be.

She had trouble putting it into words, but her mother's withdrawal also left Mid drifting. At times she felt cut off from both parents. Had Ethel Lacy been changed by the scare of that summer? Who had she been before she married Curtis and began to have children? Was there more to the story of her uncle's disappearance? How did Mid fit into this family history?

The four-year-old Mid, sick in bed, was now far away from the teenaged Marian, more like another person than herself at an earlier age. In a sense, Mid realized, that child had died. Once recovered and coming home from the lake, Marian had felt different, wise in some way children were not supposed to be and sad about the gap in her existence, the period of illness.

The girl in the poem--who was she? Marian before she got sick? The self she had become at age seventeen? An entirely different person she must still bring into being? At that moment she realized that her true self could be in the future, away and beckoning. She would have to search for that woman, outside this house or inside her imagination. She could begin tomorrow.

Chapter Two: Backwash

If there were another Marian coming into being at the Ridge Road house, one might understand how she could get lost in the crowd. Nine people generally came to Sunday dinner, but it sometimes seemed as if ghosts had come out of hiding to join them at the table.

Nana, for instance, talked about her living and dead relatives in remote German villages as if they resided on the next block and might drop by at any moment. "My aunt's stepmother, who rented rooms outside of Bodelshausen, had a spoon like this one," she might say, holding it up to the light. "I need to ask her how she keeps it so well polished." She seldom spoke, though, of her missing son, who'd left home at an early age.

Mid wondered if she'd ever go overseas like her father. What would it be like to travel down the Danube?

"You need good light to work in," observed Grandpa, squinting. "These clouds today mean a late thundershower. Hope there's no hail like the one that ruined the Williams' corn in '98." Grandpa spoke of Rutherford weather in relation to plantings and harvests on his farm, miles inland and upriver. He could not accept the fact that he would never return to the countryside.

Would she even get away from Rutherford, wondered Mid. When her grandfather moved, only John accompanied Father to Livonia. Her older brother was at the table this particular weekend when Mid was puzzling over possible other selves.

Spooning gravy onto his roast, Father caught Ethel's eye. The Deputy Escrow Officer for Argentina is Nehemiah rebuilding the wall of Jerusalem again." He often used a kind of Biblical code to communicate about his work so that only Mother understood. His comments implied, to Mid at least, that the ancient world coexisted with the present.

Knowing nothing about the object of Father's allusion, Nana nonetheless chimed in, wagging a finger at everyone. "Rome was not built in a day, they say, although I don't know who ever thought it could be."

"Fences won't keep the deer out of the tomatoes when there's not enough rain," added Grandpa, as if he'd spotted a small herd in the backyard recently.

"That Axel thinks he can storm the city walls in a day," Ella whispered to Mid. This was the most ardent of her current suitors. Ella was as skillful as Penelope in deflecting the attentions of young men without causing them to lose interest.

Was a boy Mid's means of seeing more of the world? She wasn't impressed with her male classmates at school, even those who were heading for college. Of course, more and more were looking for work in these years, the Depression pinching families and shrinking opportunities. Father had still been able to send Ella to Elmira College for her first year, and he said he wanted all of his children to complete their education.

Mid had studied pictures of flappers in fashion magazines, wishing sometimes that she had the courage to wear short dresses and dance the night away.

Mother's contributions to wandering dinner discussions were often literary and, thus, to her children indecipherable. This time she observed, *"Ah, but a man's reach should exceed his grasp, / or what's a heaven for?"* She loved the poetry of Robert Browning, but the speakers in his dramatic monologues existed in a sphere in which the rest of the family did not travel.

At the same time serious matters were being discussed, the younger children often had private campaigns of rebellion under way. "Please pass me the salt," Alice asked Bill. The shaker was almost precisely the same distance from brother and sister. But Alice was convinced that Bill, the youngest, always got preferential treatment. And she devised little tests like this to make her case, recording the results each night in a tiny journal she kept locked in the drawer of her jewelry case.

"You can reach the salt, Alice," Father said.

Alice later told Mid her reaction. "Ah-ha!" she had thought to herself, composing in her head the related journal entry: *"I am stretched to breaking so he can enjoy the best we have."*

Mid wanted to live in the here and now, 237 Ridge Road, dining room, 1:30 p.m.; but she also wanted it to mean something, to inspire her toward a fulfilling life in the future. Did each of her siblings have a clear conception of where he or she stood, who everyone else was, what the goal of their activities should be? She wanted desperately to feel that her life mattered.

"Can women join the Army?" she asked her father. "I might want to be a nurse and serve in . . . China or . . . or India."

Her Father, startled, held a forkful of pot roast six inches from his mouth. "You're going to college, Marian, like your sister. You'll find a nice boy and raise a family. Or you can stay here and help run the house with your mother."

Mid had recently read Ellen N. La Motte's *The Backwash of War*. This frank account of an American woman's service in a French field hospital during World War I had been repressed when America joined the Great War. Now that newspapers were reporting ominous developments in Germany, the work's republication was meeting with approval from groups favoring isolationism. Some worried that Hitler, the new Chancellor, might want to restore his country as a mighty military power; and a few alarmists warned that another war on the Continent was inevitable.

Mid wished for no new conflict to call her away from home, but she was moved by the strength of a woman who gave up the comforts of home to enlist in a great venture. Surely there were places where a woman's kind hands and gentle manner could accomplish good things?

"I'll go to college, too, won't I, Father?" Bill asked.

"Or course. You might even be in the business with me some day." He had been surprised when

John indicated he wanted to study engineering at the Massachusetts Institute of Technology rather than pursue a career in business.

"I want to be a missionary, after I finish my schooling. There are so many people who have never heard the Bible."

"Well, we'll see."

Curtis dismissed his second son's statements as youthful idealism. When the boy learned how hard it was--and dangerous--to deal with natives in Africa or Asia, he'd be ready to live a normal life. Not that Curtis didn't think such matters important and Christianity the one true religion; but there was plenty of God's work to be done closer to home.

Mid resented the attention her parents seemed to give the other children. The middle child--that's how she got her nickname--seemed to be a blend of the other four, not a distinct individual. Ellen LaMotte had traveled to the Orient, treating the sick, but also advancing the profession of nursing. Mid wondered if she could study medicine in college, be paid to see the other side of the world, return to the family with a new, strong identity.

She imagined herself standing in the doorway of a busy urban hospital--perhaps Bombay, or Shanghai. A tall handsome officer appears in the distance, at the end of a long narrow street. He strides purposely toward her in a scenario that reverses her father's daily departure from home to the railroad station. A train crash, the American (British?) officer announces; there are dozens-- perhaps hundreds of victims. He needs a nurse.

"You!" he orders Mid when he reaches her. "Determine the most critical; send them to me one at a time."

Handing the routine checklist she was reviewing to a native aide, she moves to the line of stretchers that hold moaning, bleeding men, women, and children. "That one," she says, "goes first. This one can wait. Put more pressure on that wound. Elevate her legs. We can do nothing for that child. Call a priest." The officer pauses for a moment to look at the striking woman. She does not turn, but knows he is watching.

In another scenario, the tall handsome man is a patient, wounded in an ugly uprising. He stayed behind to keep order in the compound while others were loaded on trucks, sent into hiding, ordered to flee. When the rebels burst through the gates, he was the only one they saw. He is brought in by two loyal natives, an arm on each one's shoulder.

"Mid, clear the table," ordered Nana.

"Bill should help," insisted Ella.

Grandpa stroked his chin thoughtfully. "I hope the netting keeps the birds out of the apples. I almost went out to look for gaps."

"He will need to be as patient as Simeon, I fear," Father concluded.

Mother agreed. "Perhaps we'll all have to wait like Dorothea Brooke."

Marian thought: I don't fit in any of these frames, but maybe I don't need to.

The life she might lead and the person she could become were transformed by that thought, though her future travel would be in a direction she did not yet envision.

Chapter Three: The Boy Next Door

There was, of course, a boy next door. And Antonio Giordano was certain he knew the woman Mid should become, regardless of any alternative self inspired by poetry, dreams, or stories in magazines. The stars he studied by telescope convinced him that the future included her as the mother of his twins.

The Lacys, who traced ancestors back to the first English settlement in this country, felt a kinship with the Giordanos, who had immigrated to the US at the end of the last century: they all were relatively new to Rutherford. Curtis had traveled from upstate New York to make his fortune, while the Giordanos were escaping more crowded neighborhoods in Bronx.

In May Antonio had been selected by his high school as one of two students to attend a summer institute in astronomy at Rutgers University. He felt manhood descend upon him the same day and vowed to take significant romantic steps toward his neighbor Mid before he left to map the sky. Mid, dreaming of a different life in Brazil or Japan, was wondering how she'd endure a final year of home economics with Miss Pearson, whose mother, according to town gossip, did all their domestic chores.

His time for departure approaching, Antonio asked Mid one early summer morning, "Are your parents close?"

"Close? Of course . . . I guess . . . I mean, they're married."

She was weeding her mother's daffodils. Mid had no idea that he raised the question of two people's togetherness with the intention of getting nearer to her.

The Lacy and Giordano children had always been close geographically, viewing their backyards as communal property. They entered the house next door with a greeting rather than a knock. And Tony and Mid, in the same class at school, sometimes did homework side by side. Scanning the neighborhood with binoculars from his upstairs bedroom, Tony had spotted Mid on her hands and knees. Pleased that she was alone, he had come out to be with her.

"I know your parents are married," he admitted. "But . . . you know . . . your dad goes into the city every day, and sometimes he doesn't get home until late. And his travel for business . . . well, your mother doesn't go with him."

Tony's father had been a trolley car conductor. Now a union official, he enjoyed a comfortable work schedule and was home a lot. Mid, with two parents, two grandparents, and four siblings, had a full house.

"Father explains where he goes and why. Mother understands his responsibilities. And when he's home, we play games together."

To talk with Tony, Mid had to look back over her shoulder. She wondered why he didn't step over to a place where she could see him.

"You . . . um . . . don't go to church together, though, do you?" The Giordanos were Catholic. While Mid's father went to a Baptist church in Newark, the children had always attended a nearby Presbyterian Sunday school on Ridge Road. Ethel's attendance was sporadic.

"You want to pull weeds?" Mid gestured toward an area she had not worked. Why was he quizzing her anyway?

Tony knelt and studied the plants before him. He kept his face averted, however, to hide a slight blush. He knew he shouldn't have been studying Mid's backside drawn tight in her khaki work clothes.

"Not here. We'll get in each other's way." She gestured. "There, by the corner."

Mid had never questioned the nature of her parents' relationship. She'd seldom heard them argue, observing, as they did, the traditional division of responsibility: she in housekeeping and (early) child rearing, he in all else. But the family always had domestic help, and, with the children well past infancy, Ethel now had leisure time that she did not spend with Curtis.

Mid knew to be careful in leaning forward that she'd didn't expose her breasts. While she'd gone through puberty late, the result was dramatic enough to catch the eyes of both male and female classmates. This pleased her for a time, as Ella had always been thought the beauty. But, a year older than many of her classmates, Mid found the boys eager to get her attention were silly at best,

25

bothersome at worst. Her true lovers existed in books, and perhaps in foreign lands.

"You know I have only one more week before the Astronomy Institute?" Tony said, pulling up a clump of false dandelion.

"That's nice."

"Well, nice that I've been selected, but not nice in that there are things I want to get done before I go."

Mid thought about the design her mother had observed in her flower beds. Daffodils, iris, small rose bushes were placed strategically by the side of the garage. Under the large maple tree, shade plants like saliva, hosta, and masterwort were separated by rocks. In selected spots by the fence were coreopsis, hydrangea, jasmine. Nothing was crowded by its neighbors or allowed to grow too large. As the season advanced, different parts of the yard were highlighted by color.

She told Tony, "We're going to the lake in another week."

While he worked, she took a hand trowel and dug around plants, loosening the soil so water would sink in with a rain. She wondered if, just for fun, she should give him a peek where her blouse gapped at the top. She was not very tall and had learned why boys sometimes tried awkwardly to stand or walk close at her side.

"It's pretty isolated up there, isn't it?" Nana and Grandpa usually looked after the Ridge Road house when they were gone.

"Sure is! Of course, my brothers and sisters, except for John, will be there. And I love to boat and swim." The main thing she didn't like at Camp Robin was trying to read by the kerosene lamps in the evening. They drew bugs and it was a strain to see. She had library volumes about Pasteur, Darwin, and Edison set aside for summer reading.

"You can really see the stars there," said Tony. "Around here there's too much city light."

"Umm." Mid pictured the vast sky reflected in Greenwood Lake. Under those heavens, who was she? Surely not the future bride of a boy she already knew! Could she wed herself to a mission instead?

She thought of her parents at the summer cabin. At first light, Father swam a steady breaststroke back and forth in front of the campsite, his morning constitutional. From her cot Mid could see, as the fog lifted, his upright head moving steadily on the dark surface. Her mother would not get up for another hour, though she was often awake reading or writing.

"They say you can find your future in the stars," Tony noted, scooting closer. "You want to know what I see up there?"

"I really need to see what's on the ground here! Watch your knee." A daffodil was in danger.

"Oops." He moved away from the flower, but ended up even nearer to Mid. "I think it would be better if I whispered it to you."

Mid sat back on her haunches, her mind on the family camp twenty-five miles away. The children slept in the cabin's main room, while her parents had a separate small room off the kitchen. They were only two dozen yards from the shore, and a hill rose directly behind the cabin to the west. Evenings were shaded, but sunrise lit up the water, half a mile across at that spot. She wondered if she could borrow a school microscope to study whatever tiny creatures were swimming in those tiny drops.

She had to admit that her father left the family for long hours every day. He had another life in the city filled with meetings, reports, study. Her mother would be lost in a book or writing letters while the children, now old enough to take care of themselves, organized their own games. They could take their small skiff anywhere on the lake. And sometimes there were other young people staying in neighboring cottages. Were they isolated beings even while living within a confined space?

Tony leaned close. "I only read my horoscope in the paper for fun, to see what it says and then compare the prediction with what really happens. Do you do that?"

"Sometimes." She pulled her head back. Why was he whispering this?

"This is what mine said today: 'Seize the day.'"

"Hm." She knew the Latin phrase and knew what he really wanted to seize.

His hip bumped hers. "Well, I think you and I should . . . Well, just in case one of the other students at the Institute has a pretty sister or something, who comes to visit him--I think you should agree to be my girlfriend, you know, before I go."

28

Mid thought two things simultaneously, one declarative and one interrogatory: "I have no desire to be this boy's girlfriend"; and "How can *I* seize the day?"

Chapter Four: Scales

In the room she shared with her sisters, Marian had a set of scales, once used, according to family legend, by an ancestor--John Lacy, shopkeeper on Nantucket. His son, Rowland H. Lacy, after a number of whaling voyages beginning when he was fifteen years old, founded the famous department store chain.

Today Mid was imagining a miniature Tony perched on one side of the balance, the man of her dreams on the other. Contradicting logic and physics, up went the material neighbor boy, down the fantasy figure. She also pictured herself on one end of a balance beam being measured against Rowland Lacy at the same age. Could she found anything?

Looking out the window past the scales, she could see the New York city skyline, the recently completed Empire State Building reaching upward beyond the New Jersey Meadows. Father would be in his office by now on his last day of work before they left for Camp Robin.

Curtis had told his children that riding the train across the swampy terrain from Rutherford to the city made him think of happy childhood days on the farm. He was suspicious of recent commissions that sought to develop this area for industry, preferring that it remain natural. Mid loved the outdoors as well and had been thrilled to go horseback riding with John and a college friend at Greenwood Lake last summer.

She also liked to go shopping in Manhattan, though, and feel a part of the hustle and bustle of urban life. She knew that some of the young women striding down sidewalks and crossing streets were secretaries, working women. While her father's staff were all male, she had learned that other officers in the company found women competent for clerical tasks . . . and that they liked having attractive women in the workplace.

Her friend Stella had told a lurid tale of her cousin's boss demanding she stay late to prepare reports. "He'd send out for dinner," said Stella. "And it came with a bottle of wine." Later, he said he was going to divorce his wife. But it turned out she owned the company.

Mid knew Stella could exaggerate, but at least that secretary had some excitement in her life. And couldn't she always have said "no" and left?

She heard Ella stirring in her bed. She'd been out with Axel Swenson the night before, her most persistent suitor, who worked in his father's dredging business. He had explained the process to Ella, and Mid then heard more than she wanted about spoils, bed levelers, and suction.

"Where's Alice?" Ella asked.

"Nana has her." Ella smiled, knowing that an extended sewing lesson would fill their younger sister's day. She and Mid had been graduated from apprentice status and were allowed to work without direction, so long as they met their grandmother's deadlines.

"Good." Ella sprang from her bed and moved a chair next to the dressing table where Mid was sitting. "Oh, Mid, you'll never guess what!"

"You've decided to join the Foreign Legion?"

"No, silly. It's not that at all. Wherever do you get such ideas? No. The fact is . . . the fact is, Axel and I are going to get married!"

"That's wonderful, Ella. He's such an earnest boy." Mid knew that she'd been out with him quite a few times in the weeks since she'd come home from college. They'd known each other in high school, but Mid thought Ella enjoyed keeping all the boys guessing about her intentions. And there was plenty of time for her to change her mind.

"You don't understand, Mid: we're getting married *this* summer."

"This summer? But, you can't do that. He has no money, no place for you to live. Why, Father says there may not be even be any city funds for dredging in the future."

While the Lacy family had not suffered greatly in these hard times, they all knew about bank closings, bread lines, Hoovervilles in the Western states. Thinking about Ella and Axel married brought the reality of economic struggle into sharper focus.

"We don't care, Mid. We're in love. Ax says he can provide for me. And . . . and . . . I could work if we needed some extra money. I just . . . don't want to be away from him."

"Work? There are no jobs for you. And won't you go back to Elmira? Father won't like it if you don't finish college. Has Ax spoken to him yet?"

Ella frowned. "Not yet. He's going to come to the lake next weekend. He'll ask . . . then."

Mid wondered if it were selfish to think what it might be like if Ella moved out. She would have more space, and, being less close in age to Alice, she would enjoy a new independence.

"Will you talk with Mother?" Mid asked.

"Should I?"

Mid recalled the story of how her mother had met Curtis Lacy. Ethel and Nana were living in a boarding house in Brooklyn after Mr. Woodruff passed away. They had little to live on and weren't sure what the future held. The brother, Henry, was already estranged from his mother, though Mid never knew when that split began or where Henry was at the time. He appeared--and disappeared!--in her family history only at the point of the supposed train accident.

Ethel had noticed an energetic young man walking by every day, surely on his way to and from work. She found reasons to be in front of the boarding house at convenient times--polishing the doorknob, studying the little wire gate to see if a bit of oil would keep it from squeaking, making sketches of houses across the street. A friendly smile would lead to a polite "hello." Soon, Curtis was scheduling more time for his walks to the train station and back.

Ella had never needed to do anything to have boys want to be near her. Her rich red hair alone was a beacon. And she had a gift for chatter that put them all at ease, though there was substance beneath her laugh and her small talk. She kept enough of her thoughts hidden that no admirers were scared away.

Mid did not have the same skills, frequently deflating a potential admirer by contradicting casual observations or questioning superficial assumptions. She had barely stopped herself with Tony when he'd suggested his summer studies could bring him into contact with another young woman. He wanted Mid to understand such a person as a rival. "Oh," she had almost said, "with all those telescopes they have at the Institute, she would see right through you."

In this case, she had fortuitously fallen back on an ancient formula: "Let's write to each other--every day. That way I'll know what you're doing, and you can picture me up at the Lake. At the end of summer, it will almost be as if we haven't been apart." She was pretty sure he'd be consumed by his studies in astronomy, safely lost in other galaxies while she continued to plot her own future on the ground--as much as was possible.

"You *have* to talk to Mother," Mid insisted to Ella. "You'll need her help to have any chance. Father won't approve at first--you know, because of the money. They say more people are out of work every day now. And Ax won't be able to continue night school if he's laid off." Ella's suitor was taking courses in electrical engineering, hoping to rise in the work force.

Ella knelt at Mid's side. "*You* could speak for me. Everyone listens to you; you're so sensible."

Mid tried not to grimace. But she *was* sensible! She conformed to expectations, she didn't contradict convention, she never took sides. But the sensible, mature life she was adopting did not offer excitement. She told her sister, "Being sensible is waiting a few years, until Ax has a steady income, a place of his own. Didn't you tell me he wants to get out of the dredging business?"

Ella pouted. "He should have been able to go to college. He's so smart, but his dad can't help him. And he has two brothers who will have to find jobs, and a sister to marry off."

Mid thought of herself as a sister to be married off. Alice, too. Bill could study anything he liked, just like John, and take a job in San Francisco, if he wanted. Would Father even let her work in his company? She had made As in shorthand and dictation.

She told Ella, "You talk to Mother. I'm not sure I won't agree with Father."

If the tall handsome doctor of her dreams had called her sweetheart and told her to come with him to China, she'd have packed her suitcase that morning--or so she thought. She said to Ella, "Would you want to live with his family? Do they even have room for one more?"

Ella groaned and ran back to the bed, pulling the covers up over her head. Mid turned around to look at the scales on the little table by the window. She pictured Ax and Ella in a one-room apartment, shivering against the winter cold. At the other end of the scales was a well-dressed, prosperous couple, both with college degrees.

She pictured herself balanced on a boss's knee, pencil poised over her stenographer's pad. He swung his leg up and down, and she rode it sidesaddle. That fantasy was never fulfilled.

Still, not that many years later, her director, a doctor, did go down on his knee and ask for her hand.

Chapter 5: How Tall, How Far, How Deep?

After the Lacys had been at Greenwood Lake for a week, the familiar routine was established. Ella, however, preparing for her suitor's arrival, was making a special effort to help her mother. The younger sisters were hoping for summer romance.

"How tall is he?" whispered Alice, squinting down the lake to the dock on the other side of the cove. It was evening, and with the wind from the south, their voices might carry, making the unknown man gazing out over the water feel that they were right beside him.

"Tall!" was all Mid could say. It was hard to estimate with nothing but the lake's surface and a far shore to measure him against. Even as distant as they were, though, she had remarked his lean form, an angular posture.

Mid wondered if she should get the binoculars from the shelf by the wood stove and if she'd be caught spying should the stranger turn in their direction. The man's silhouette shimmered an invitation out at the point, but right now she was not unhappy to fill in the outline of a man with her own specifications.

She was reluctant to initiate contact on the eve of Ax's arrival. On Sunday the dredge operator's son was to request Mr. Lacy's permission to ask for Ella's hand. Mid anticipated fireworks that might spread out to affect any potential love interests of her own.

"Let's go up the hill and sneak down for a closer look," Alice suggested, nudging Mid with an elbow. "We can take the path by the cave."

Since they arrived, they'd seen only a few of the usual other residents at cottages scattered along the shore to the north. Right now Bill was somewhere with Steven, a boy who lived here year round. His father ran Long's passenger launch to and from the little train station on the east bank of the lake. Father, who left early every morning for work, would be home soon for a long weekend.

When all the summer people had established themselves, there would sometimes be dozens of playfellows ready to join the Lacys in Kick the Can or Steal the Flag, especially on holiday weekends. The Stuart house, however, had been boarded up for as long as the Lacys had been coming to Greenwood Lake.

Mid glanced behind her, noting that the sun had already disappeared behind the ridge. It would soon be dark down where they were, remaining light up on the hill for half an hour more. By climbing, they would go back in time; and then, coming down, they could skip forward to the present. They knew the path to the cave well, as it was a favorite hideout in games when other children were in the area.

"Okay," Mid said. "But we can't give ourselves away. The light will be behind us." She jumped to her feet and trotted past the old stone grill on the edge of the woods. Cool air descended the hillside as evening approached and brushed their faces as they climbed.

Mid thought of the Blythe sisters in one of her favorite stories series. Before they encountered hardships in the big city, they had enjoyed an idyllic childhood on Long Island. In some of the books, they would return to the country for vacations, where they inevitably encountered swindlers who had to be outsmarted, blizzards that involved them with mysterious strangers, lost girls who needed friends. What would she and Alice find at the Stuart home, unoccupied for years, but now apparently full of guests?

Nearing Funnel Cave, Mid worried that it would be too dark to see when they approached the other house. The point was several hundred yards away from their camp as the crow flies, or as a boat travels; but the route they were taking was circuitous and winding. The journey would take longer than Alice had thought.

"Hurry," Mid told her sister, who was falling behind.

"I'll . . . catch up . . . " she panted. "You go . . .. ahead."

Mid reached the cave and waited. A trickle of water bubbled from the mouth of the cave, itself so deep no one had found an end to it. Alice loved the fantasy that, if you crawled far enough, you could come out in another valley--or end up in Wonderland! Mid worried that her own travel had no destination. Funnel Cave also reminded her of the Missouri cave Tom Sawyer roamed around in, though it was not nearly so big inside. Instead of huge rooms and multiple passages, it shrank down after about twenty yards to a tunnel (or funnel) less than three feet high.

Waiting for Alice, she wondered if she would ever see natural wonders like Twain's Mississippi River in the Show Me State. Traveling out of the country would be like falling into the rabbit hole, meeting characters and encountering situations unimagined in her regular life.

"Be careful not to make noise," she whispered to Alice, who had come up behind her.

They started moving faster now, though both girls tried to slow themselves by holding on to saplings and pushing back on tree trunks. There were lights in windows at the back of the house. And, as high as they were, they saw, over the roof, small waves coming toward shore, illuminated by porch light.

"Go down the lane," urged Alice. It ran along the shore and back to their own camp. From there they might study the stranger--or strangers--and then race home.

A radio was playing through an open window. Wasn't that Cab Calloway doing "Minnie the Moocher"? Mid couldn't be sure, as this kind of music was considered revolutionary by her parents. She only heard it at friends' houses.

They were on the side of the road next to the bank, trying to find a place to view the porch and the dock. The wind had shifted to the east, so the sound of a screen door's opening drifted to them, followed by an odd, soft "ka-thump." Then they spotted the tall man they'd seen from their camp; he was backing across the porch pulling something--a carton or trash can or some piece of furniture. No, it was someone in a wheelchair. Once across the porch, he turned it around, tilted it back, and lowered it carefully down the steps to the dock. More "ka-thumps."

Mid had seen only one wheelchair in her life. An elderly invalid in a house near Dr. Paterson on Ridge Road would be taken to Lincoln Park to feed the pigeons on mild days. The cane chair creaked as its frame was twisted by uneven ground.

"Who is that?" whispered Alice, grabbing Mid's hand. She didn't know if Alice meant the person in the chair or the man who was pulling it.

"What a glorious night, Syd," said a voice out on the dock. It was probably the person in the chair speaking, as it didn't sound like a man's voice. The passenger, whose back was toward the girls, presented only a shadow against the water. Then she began to sing with the radio music: *she had a dream about the King of Sweden / he gave her things that she was needin'* ."

Mid shivered. What were the things a man could give that a woman would need? She recalled Tony bumping his hip against her in the flower garden. She knew all about boys wanting to kiss, but this contact had been different. And he was breathing funny when he talked about seizing the day. She should ask Ella if Ax did things like that.

She also wondered if she would ever go to Sweden, so far to the north and across the sea? She'd

41

seen pictures of Scandinavian fjords and learned about their short winter days with long, cold nights. Grandpa told her once about ice caves north of Greenwood Lake, somewhere across the border in New York. He said on the Fourth of July you could find blocks of ice in the deep recesses of rock. It was winter long after the time you were accustomed to it.

The deeper voice of the man sang the refrain to Cab Calloway's song: *"hidey-hi's, one mo' 'gain!) / poor min, poor min, poor min!"*

Was it Minnie or the girl in the wheelchair he was singing about, poor Minnie? Was this the man's sister? His mother? How would she, unable to travel, know this kind of music?

Then, behind her over the water, she heard the deep toll of the camp bell, hung from the eave by their cabin's front door. It had been at Grandpa's farm, one of the few things he'd saved for which they could find a use. Whenever the children heard it, they were to come home. This time it probably meant that Father had arrived and dinner would come soon.

"Come on, Alice," she said, pulling on her sister's arm. But her sister was mesmerized by the scene on the dock, the singing and the music.

"Wait! Look," she whispered. "He's going to kiss her."

And Mid could see the tall form bending over the seated one, his arms go around the other's neck. In the dark it looked more like a hug than a kiss, but it was impossible to tell.

42

The farm bell sounded again, this time, it seemed, more urgently. Mid scanned the shore across the cove, but could see nothing except the hillside rising from the lake's surface and the cabin windows, lit by the kerosene lanterns inside. Then she heard her father shout, "Bill! Bill! where are you?" She'd only heard panic in his voice once. But now she heard it again.

Chapter Six: Distress Call

Racing into the light on the camp porch, Mid and Alice were confronted by Ella and their mother. "Where is Bill? Have you seen him?"

"We don't know. Wasn't he with Steven?"

Ethel explained that Steven's father, piloting the last launch of the evening, with Curtis Lacy aboard, had found a canoe paddle floating in the lake. They'd hallo'd across the water but heard no response. The girls were either too intent on their adventure, or making too much noise as they hiked, to hear them calling. They were lost in their own adventure. Still, whoever was in the canoe should have had another paddle.

Curtis had no idea Bill might have been out on the water until Ethel told him she wasn't sure where he was. "He's with Mid and Alice . . . I think." He decided he'd better find out.

Ethel later confessed that she'd not been attentive to what was going on around her, absorbed instead in Tennyson's *The Princess.* With current discussions about the rise of Fascism in Europe on her mind, she was wondering if Ida's dream of an ideal society had ended with The Great War. She was worlds away from Greenwood Lake

Curtis rang the farm bell, hoping for a quick response from all his children. Hearing no answers, he rang it almost brutally. When the sisters arrived, he wished he'd gone in the launch with Mr. Long, who'd borrowed an extra lantern and was motoring slowly to the middle of the lake. They could all hear him calling out, though the sound was muffled and indistinct.

Then they heard shouting from across the cove. A young person was calling, "Bill! Bill, where are you?" Then someone announced in a deeper, rasping voice, "I've got him. Help me up on the shore."

The Lacys ran up the road, Father outpacing the rest. They were going back the way Mid and Alice had come, Ethel the slowest, gasping for air, holding her side, trying to pray.

At last they came into a circle of light around the Stuart house, where several more lanterns had been hung from the porch ceiling. Perhaps half a dozen people were clustered at the top of the steps; the person in the wheelchair was not visible. Mid could see Father kneeling on the bank, holding someone's head in his lap. Was it Bill?

"He's okay, Mother. He's okay," said Father, though Mid could see that fear had not left his face. The tall man she'd seen earlier was leaning on the porch railing. He took out a cigarette and struck a match. His face, illuminated by the flame, was as handsome as Mid had imagined.

The boys, it turned out, had "borrowed" a canoe from one of the unoccupied cottages and gone exploring. Some sort of confusion occurred, and a paddle went overboard. Using the remaining paddle, they chased after it on a circuitous route. When Bill finally found himself close, he lunged out for it. But he had misjudged its location in the growing darkness and went in headfirst, rocking the canoe. His friend overreacted and, trying to balance, fell in on the other side of the boat.

Steven, assuming there was no great danger, arrived at the Stuart's dock before he realized Bill wasn't with him. When the tall man heard there was another person in the water, he pulled off his shoes and swam out to where Steven pointed. Within minutes he had fished the boy out of the water.

Bill was sitting up now, coughing and looking sheepish. "I must have bumped my head when the canoe flipped. Maybe it was the paddle. The next thing I knew . . . this . . . this man had me by the shirt collar."

Ethel, kneeling beside him, cried softly. "You must never go out like that again. Your uncle . . . " She stopped abruptly. "It was getting dark; you should have come in."

Mid felt guilty about the accident. She was not supposed to be responsible for her brother, but she knew it was assumed they all kept an eye on each other. She had been chasing a Blythe sisters fantasy when Bill almost drowned.

"We owe you our deepest gratitude . . . ?" Curtis reached out to shake the hand of the rescuer. It was clear he didn't know who this man was. Mid studied his linen trousers, still neat after being in the lake.

"Sydney Stuart." He shrugged. "I only did what anyone would. Fortunately, I found him quickly."

Curtis looked up at the people gathered on the porch, presumably the larger Stuart family. "It's lucky you all were here. I don't think we've ever seen the house occupied."

An elderly, well dressed man stepped down to meet him. "Moncrief. We're from Providence. But you're right, we've not been down for many years. There's a man, " he gestured vaguely, "in, um, Monroe, who checks on the place a few times each year."

"Curtis Lacy, my wife Ethel, my children. We have a little cabin . . . " He pointed down the shore. "You must let us bring you some vegetables. We raise spinach, lettuce, broccoli." He smiled with satisfaction, thinking even then of his childhood on a farm.

Mr. Stuart smiled. "No, no. We have brought provisions . . . and we have a cook." Again, the gesture of pointing, but without specificity.

"Well, should you need anything . . . finding things locally, do let us help. Again, we're so grateful your son . . . ?" Mr. Stuart nodded slightly in his direction. " . . . was so alert, so prompt in his assistance."

Mid noted that Father's language had changed, adapting to the other man's style. She'd not heard him speak like that except, occasionally, in business telephone calls from their home to the city. She exchanged questioning glances with Ella, who seemed to have noticed also.

The Lacys said farewell, each of them nodding or echoing the head of the household's gratitude, and they returned to Camp Robin. Mid felt lessened by the experience, not just at her brother's needing

47

rescue but by the other family's manner. Still, she wondered if the second major romantic prospect in her life had opened up when she met the Stuart family.

Later that night, when they were supposed be asleep, Bill told Alice and Ella what it had been like to go under the water.

"I got disoriented. I didn't know which way was up or down. I could have been a foot below the surface or deeper than I've ever dived. I couldn't tell where I was or, at one point, who I was."

All the children were excellent swimmers. And Bill especially loved the challenge of going after interesting items spotted from the dock or a boat. The bottoms of some lakes in this region, bordered by high hills, could be hundreds of feet down. The farther you descended, the colder the water, which can slow responses and dull thinking. Greenwood Lake, after a dam built in 1837 increased its size, was nearly sixty feet deep at some points.

Mid wanted to put an arm around Bill or console him in some way. But she sensed his pride wouldn't allow it.

"The water can be cloudy, too. So you probably couldn't see to get your bearings." Unwillingly, she found herself almost resenting that his actions had made him the center of attention.

"I thought the canoe was the bottom of the lake. It was really just a shadowy shape. I must have been practically right up under it. I couldn't see around it, so I swam the other way."

She remembered being sick with the flu, ten or twelve years ago. Somewhere between sleeping and waking, she'd been unable able to fix herself in dream or reality. Now she wondered if, struggling toward consciousness like Bill, her true self had been lost or found in that strange space between worlds.

Bill went on. "I heard Steven calling, I think, but it was muffled. Water got in my ears, and it was like he was in another room or in the attic two stories above me. I guess, I must have blacked out."

Bill's account made Mid think of the one transatlantic phone call she had received. Her father, away for several months on a business trip, had telephoned from London, speaking for less than a minute to each of his children. Curtis' voice faded in and out as it was being relayed by radio transmission, which was frequently affected by atmospheric disturbance.

Father's words coming and going made him seem to be materializing and disappearing, just as, when she'd been ill, her conscious self traded places with a dreaming self. Hearing Father clearly in one moment, Mid felt he could be next door or perhaps in the city. When interference rose and his voice faded, she understood he was across an ocean.

Recalling her separation from Father sadly made her remember his separation from his own parent.

Chapter Seven: Deliveries

Bringing the paper in from the Ridge Road front porch on October 29, 1929, Curtis Lacy's mother suffered a fatal stroke. She and her husband had taken the train down from Rochester, intending to stay only a few days. She went home to be buried.

Grandpa returned to the farm for less than a year after that, finding it too hard to work on his own and the harsh winter too much to bear with no relatives close by.

The family accepted the idea that that day's headlines--"Hysterical Liquidation Sinking Prices"--caused Ella's collapse. The Lacys were of stern New England stock, believing in self reliance. Nothing inside their hardworking bodies could bring on failure, but the corrupt action of people far removed might. So, what she read in the paper was deemed the deathblow.

Years later, of course, the grandchildren understood that she had suffered for years from coronary heart disease. It was more likely that walking up the steps, not distant economic malfeasance, was the final strain that brought on Grandmother's stroke.

All five children saw their father when he came home from the city. Ethel's urgent telephone call had interrupted a meeting, and he came immediately. The family witnessed how strain had tightened every facial feature, and his eyes glittered with intensity. Grandmother lingered for a week, but never regained consciousness, her mind wandering, it was believed, in recollections of her Quaker childhood.

When Mid later came upon her father on his knees by the Stuart house with a child in his arms, the memory of that earlier event flashed before her eyes. A parent's vulnerability scars a child's heart. She had never been able conceive of the patriarch as uncertain of himself, and she had buried that memory of him deep in her consciousness.

Bill came up from the depth of the lake, however, thanks to a stranger's hand. And Curtis Lacy revived. It didn't seem fair that the next shock--Axel's announcements--should come so quickly. Nor did it seem right that Mid would have to confront a crisis of her own on a vacation that was supposed to open into romantic adventure.

She understood that Sydney Stuart, aristocrat of Rhode Island, was not someone she would have met in her small world of Rutherford, New Jersey. He was the kind of man she had read about in novels by George Eliot or Henry James, scion of European dynasties. Should he ever be face to face with a businessman's daughter, would he seek further contact?

"What happened to the girl in the chair?" Alice asked the next day. The three sisters were getting ready to swim out to the floating platform their older brother had installed several years earlier. It was anchored to a sunken stone pier once used for docking steamboats.

"Girl?" asked Ella. Mid and Alice had not told her about sneaking up on the Stuarts. They agreed it would be prudent to conceal exactly where they had been at the time of the accident.

"Oh, Alice thought she saw a wheelchair as we ran up," said Mid, signaling her with a stern look. Then, thinking back, she added, "If there was someone in a wheelchair, she must have been behind those people on the porch, or inside. Stress would never be good for an invalid."

"What would she have to worry about?" Alice sighed. "That handsome brother . . . or whatever he was . . . could take care of anything." Ella's eyebrows went up. Lowering her voice, Alice added, "Did you seen the muscles in his arms? And how broad his chest was?"

Mid had admired the man, too, his wet shirt outlining a lean physique. But late to appreciate masculine beauty herself, she didn't think Alice old enough to be pay attention in this way. She looked to Ella for confirmation, but the older sister was gazing out over the lake.

Perhaps it was because Mid's own development was slow that she felt the gap between her and her younger sister should be greater. Alice's bathing suit made it clear she had already entered womanhood, at least physically. Which girl would a stranger find more attractive?

"Let's race to the raft!" challenged Alice. They hopped over the pebbly shore and splashed into the water, still cold from the lake's depth and the long winter. The chill was invigorating.

Mid reached the ladder half a stroke ahead, the closest she'd ever come to losing. "Still the fastest!" she gasped, but wondered if she could hold that title forever.

The girls climbed up on the platform and peeled off their bathing caps, ready to lie in the warm sun and escape possible chores. Their parents were concentrating on Bill anyway, convinced he should have a day of rest despite his sullen protests. Mid and Alice had woken up daydreaming about their new neighbors and were eager to return to their fantasies.

Mid especially wondered about the girl in the wheelchair, who sang "Minnie the Moocher" so beautifully. It was strange that she could travel this far. Did they have a special automobile? Did they lift her in and out of the chair to get her in the house? Could she walk a little bit?

Mid was dozing when she heard the launch chugging out from the opposite shore. After the morning commuters, Mr. Long seldom had passengers to ferry. Was this something about yesterday's canoe theft?

Years ago steamboats capable of carrying several hundred passengers operated in this area. The Greenwood Lake Transportation Company owned the *Milford*, the *Arlington* and a side wheeler, *Montclair*, with two decks. When trains came in, the boats ferried them to resorts around the lake in New Jersey and New York. The power of steam brought every place closer.

A few minutes later, a familiar voice called out, "Good afternoon, Lacy ladies!" It was Axel Swenson. They saw him up at the bow in his best clothes and carrying flowers. Ella gave a shy wave and slipped back into the water. She would receive those roses from him on shore.

The flowers, though, were for Mrs. Lacy. Axel had something for Mid also. She could see immediately it was a letter from Tony and tucked it out of sight.

Axel's arrival was ill-timed, as both parents were still unsettled after yesterday's events. A declaration of love might have been better received a week or more later. But his proposal was more specific than a general intention to court: he wanted Ella to marry him this summer.

"Out of the question," Father said, barely containing his shock at such boldness. "How would you support her? And I want her to finish her education. She's still a child."

Ella reddened but kept her tongue. She was letting the man she loved speak for her.

"Begging your pardon, sir, but Ella is far more mature than young ladies five, or even ten years older. And we're not like you in believing we have to wait until we're completely established to become one. We want to get ahead together."

This wasn't exactly accurate, as he was implying she was about to join the work force. Ella would learn later, with some pain, that he was too proud ever to admit he would need income from his wife. He kept a strict division between the sexes.

"We're in a recession, young man! People are begging for jobs. What makes you think you're going to have an income for a family in times like these? Why, you're as far away from being the head of a household as I am from . . . from the other end of the lake."

Father was also contradicting himself. He'd always insisted that hard work and a proper attitude would be rewarded in America. In this case, he wanted to assert the opposite.

Then Axel dropped his bombshell. "I have a job in Maine, Sir, beginning in September. In a year or two, Ella and I will be able to buy a house. For now, I am simply requesting permission to ask for your daughter's hand in marriage so that she can accompany me this fall."

"You do not have it, young man! And please leave this . . . " He wanted to say "house," but, of course, the cabin plus tented extensions was not a manor from which he could deliver lofty dismissals. "And please live this . . . this area . . . immediately."

Long's launch had crossed back to the far shore, so Axel had difficulty following Curtis' demand immediately. And he wanted to talk to Ella. But Curtis stepped between them with his arms crossed.

Mid, always the conciliator, took Axel's arm and guided him toward the landing, promising quietly to help their cause. Privately, she didn't want her sister in Maine, to her as far away as the moon. She also felt she should be the one to travel!

Mid wanted to help end the quarrel not only to restore harmony in the family but also so she could read Tony's letter, presumably mailed from the Astronomy Institute. Despite promises to write to her, he'd sent only a few innocuous postcards. This was fine, in general, giving her breathing room to consider other boys--and other futures. Still, attention was flattering even if you didn't intend to respond to it.

Tony's interest in her, expressed with surprising energy in this letter, complicated her summer in a small way. At the very least, she had to keep it secret from Father, already worried about one of his daughters. When she was in college just a few years later, though, the former "boy next door" became a major part of her destiny. And a few more years after that, as the world was being torn apart in war, he would renew his courtship in a startlingly convincing way.

Chapter Eight: Voices

"*I've decided to join the fight for workers overseas,*" Tony wrote. "*I want you to marry me before I do.*" Mid smiled when she read the first sentence and grimaced when she read the second.

Tony went on to explain how gazing at the heavens for the past few weeks had made him think about his life in "the grand scheme of history." Things were happening in Europe, and he thought the time was coming when America would be involved in another foreign conflict. One of the teachers at the Institute was a veteran who'd seen service in the Great War; and democracy, he said, would need new heroes. And every hero needs a sweetheart back home.

Mid was impressed that Tony's ambition had gone from the local to the global. But that didn't mean she had to marry him so that he could save the free world. And, of course, that would mean becoming Catholic.

Catholics worshipped the Pope in Rome and trappings from the Middle Ages, Father had told her many times, not the living Christ in our midst. They recited phrases in Latin without ever reading the Bible. How could you be truly born again if the church simply heard your confession, handed out penance, and awarded you absolution--no matter what was in your heart?

She reread Tony's letter. "*I will never want another woman to be my wife. And I would go crazy living a conventional life in Rutherford. Colonel Romero says I won't be a man unless I'm willing to risk death in the service of a cause. Think of me somewhere fighting oppression if you can't think of me at home with you."*

Well, at least Tony might see some of the world as a soldier, thought Mid enviously. If she decided to volunteer for something like that, it would turn out there was a post for her in Lyndhurst! And she was not going to see the world as a military wife. Tony might give her a daughter and then get himself killed in some Godforsaken battlefield. Where would she be then?

Out on the lake the wind had shifted, and she thought she heard music, a jazz vocal. She turned toward the window, open to let in cool air. It must be the Stuarts, that girl in the wheelchair.

Her father's anger haunted her, but the letter from Tony, now tucked away in her diary, also made sleeping difficult. Mid wished she could magically freeze the lake and skate away from her problems. She would have liked to fly on up the lake with powerful strides, ice chips in her wake as she had back in February.

The Lacy children swam and boated on Greenwood Lake in the warm summer months, sometimes leisurely and on other occasions in contests of speed. But every once in a while in the winter, they also ice skated. In her last such cold weather excursion, Mid found that distances shrank and time collapsed.

She and John had joined Father for a Saturday's escape after he announced he had breathed too much city smoke, enduring too many days without sunshine, and been trapped in small spaces for too many hours in a row. They were in the midst of an especially cold winter, and the lake surface was solid enough to drive a car on.

When they pulled into Camp Robin, ice lay under the firs, spread out from the shore, ran along creeks frozen in their descents down hillsides. While their father checked the cabin for leaks and places that might need repair, John and Mid laced on their skates and started north to study the frozen landscape.

John liked to imagine engineering projects that he might undertake in the future: bridges across even such wide expanses of water, tunnels through mountains, trams that would take tourists to lookout spots on the hills. Mid was watching for living creatures that might be moving close to the shore.

When her brother paused at an old ferry landing on the shore opposite Camp Robin, contemplating the possibility of installing a fishing pier for tourists reaching out into the lake, Mid leisurely cut a few figure eights nearby. She wondered if she could write a message that could be viewed from an airplane overhead. Or from the stars. If so, what would she say?

After a while, realizing that John was lost in meditation, Mid skated off on her own. The trees and creek mouths slid past her, the ice at the perfect temperature to convert to water beneath her blades. She marveled at the northern shore rising up at her across the lake, Camp Robin receding behind her.

She was moving at ten times the speed of their canoe or of swimming.

The lake was so still that all she heard was the slice and dig of her own skates, the turning of the toe to get traction, the lift at the end of each stroke, a hypnotic rhythm in a steady song of speed. Her legs sent her forward effortlessly.

At one point, Mid thought she heard another skater behind her or perhaps out of sight in different part of the lake. Still skating, she glanced back over one shoulder, then the other; but she could see no one. She leaned into the journey again, breathing deeply.

After a few more minutes, she was sure she heard it again, another pair of blades rhythmically echoing hers somewhere. She stopped and pivoted slowly in a complete circle, searching through the shadows where creeks had cut their paths to bigger water. In the bright light she located John as a dark dot far off in the distance, not moving. She supposed he was envisioning the construction of an entire business. Who else was out there?

This summer night, her reverie of that winter gliding was broken by a haunting voice floating over the water supported by the chords of a mournful piano: "*Back Water Blues that calls me to pack my things and go.*"

She raised her head from the pillow and listened to see if anyone else was awake. Easy breathing by her brother and sisters. Nothing from behind the door of her parents room. She slipped off the cot and went to the window.

"*Mmm, I can't move no more/ Mmm, I can't move no more / There ain't no place for a poor old girl to go.*" Mid had no place to go, no one besides Tony thinking of her as a sweetheart.

She tiptoed through the screen door out onto their porch. There was no moon, but the stars arched over the lake marking a path to the house of the tall man. She saw a Milky Way to romance. How could she become a shooting star and cut her own path across that galaxy?

She thought about putting on her clothes, hiking up the shore road. It might take ten minutes to reach that music, very little time, really, to leave the Lacys and be with another family. Ella might make a much greater move this fall, marrying and moving to Maine, while Mid was still at Rutherford High School, studying to cook and sew and raise children. How long would it take to be the nurse who captivated a doctor overseas?

Well, she would have to finish high school, graduate from nursing school, get her training in a hospital. And the travel alone was overwhelming. She saw it all as a question in a science class: "If a train passenger left New York bound for Los Angeles at 9:00 on an autumn morning, traveling at 50 miles per hour through Pittsburgh, St. Louis, Oklahoma City, and Albuquerque, when would she board the ship for New Zealand where she would meet her lover?" And when, thought Mid, would that lover realize he had married a saint?

The singer's voice sank to a soft humming; the radio music faded in the woods and hills surrounding the lake. Mid imagined her neighbors summoning servants to turn down beds, arrange clothes for the morning, take their posts for the night. Her family was far removed from that life. While they did have a cook at home, the children were assigned household chores and the parents believed that every person was responsible for his person.

She saw a small red light glowing between her and the other house. It seemed to be jiggling or shaking. A cigarette probably, but who, Mid wondered, was smoking it? It's Axel, she thought. He's haunting the place where Ella lies sleeping. If Father wakes up, there'll be another difficult scene.

Could it be Sydney? When he had leaned against the porch, he had the look of melancholy, a man who, unable to sleep from a sense of ennui, would walk at night. The burdens of his position might be understood and accepted, but they did not inspire the latest heir to a fortune. A wisdom beyond his years and an artistic sensibility cut him off from the privileged role passed down from generation to generation. Or so Mid speculated.

Then she heard someone whisper her name. Bill must have seen her getting up. He was beside her, but looking up at the stars, not toward the little red dot of light.

"Mid," he said, "Mid, down in the water, in the dark, do you know what else I saw? The hand of God reached down to save me. I was as close to Him as I am to you. And I'm committing myself to Him.

You have to help me figure out how to tell Father I am going to be a missionary."

And once more, Mid found the question of her destiny dwarfed by another's.

"That boy in the wheelchair up at the Stuarts," said Ethel to Bill several days later. "Have you made friends with him?"

Boy in a wheelchair, wondered Mid. There was a boy, too?

She was sunning with her sisters on the raft and overheard their conversation. Bill was paddling his mother about on a gentle canoe ride. Father was in the city and, because he had to meet with a branch officer in Boston on Wednesday, would not return until Friday.

"Mother, I just met him."

"He seemed a very nice young man, and I bet he could use a friend, having to stay in that chair. Maybe he'd like to play chess."

Mid saw that Alice was listening, too. "Did you see a boy?" she whispered. With everyone so worried about Bill, she had retained only fragmented images of the Stuart family up on the porch. The clearest pictures in her head were the ones of Sydney.

"No," Alice told Mid. "Unless . . . "

"Unless?"

"Mid," interrupted Ella. "When Mr. Long came across this morning, did he say anything or leave anything?"

Ella had stayed in bed for an extra hour after a restless night. Mid, awake early, had watched the ferry come and go.

"Father got on board just like he always does. I didn't hear if they said anything. It all seemed routine."

She didn't tell Ella that Mr. Long had passed an envelope to Father, who glanced at it and then tucked it into his briefcase. A letter from Axel, no doubt, but whether it had been addressed to him or Ella was impossible to tell.

Alice said, "Even if he had a letter from Ax, Father would have confiscated it. You might as well think of yourself as under house arrest!"

"I won't be a prisoner here," Ella pouted. "If I have to, I'll run away. We could elope, you know."

Mid didn't think Ax would put a ladder to the upstairs bedroom window at the Ridge Road house and have Ella climb down with a single bag of worldly belongings. While he was sure of himself, like so many Scandinavians, he also respected tradition. He'd wear Father down with his determination. Ella would have to learn patience.

She replayed in her mind Father's departure that morning. The lake was so still that the ferry seemed to be stationary even as it dwindled in size and melted into a misty shore. Again, Mid stayed fixed in one place while her father receded into other worlds.

"Paddle me up to the Stuarts', Bill," Mother said. "We'll offer to have a picnic, where the shore has such big rocks."

"Smelters' Point?"

"Yes, if that's what you call it." Mother seldom left the campsite, so this proposal surprised her children. She pointed. "Isn't that it, right there? It will be shady by the middle of the afternoon."

Ella called from the raft, "I'm not sure they're the kind of people who picnic."

"Unless it's on a yacht," whispered Mid. "Or the rooftop of a penthouse."

Ethel either didn't hear them or pretended she didn't. She and Bill drifted north, propelled by his paddling and a slight breeze.

Smelter's Point was famous locally as a romantic getaway for ironworkers of the last century. In the late 1700s, several hundred families were brought from Germany to build and operate a furnace on the Wanaque River, south of Greenwood Lake (then known as Long Pond). The work was hard but prosperous, for a time. The close community continued to speak German and preserve Old World traditions.

Mid thought of those immigrants, perhaps sad to leave their homeland but excited at new opportunities. She'd learned from her history classes that Europe was a continent racked by long wars and oppression by corrupt monarchies. Many would want a chance to start over in a New World. Was her own condition far from theirs?

She imagined Bill in Africa, preaching to dark-skinned, unclothed natives in a steamy jungle where wild beasts roared at night. Would the chance to leave material comforts and a free society be as attractive as he imagined?

When the market dropped in the early nineteenth century, most of the German ironworkers of the Ramapo Mountains moved south to Pennsylvania. But some descendants stayed in the area, adopting American ways and marrying outside of their tight knit circle. Local legend maintained that proposals to non-German women occurred at Smelters' Point, a safe distance from parents. Those marriages produced the next generation, who developed this region for tourism. Their trains and steamboats brought wealthy city residents to vacation in the mountains.

Music was coming from the Stuarts' cottage again, the easy dance of jazz. Mid remembered what her younger sister had said earlier. "Alice, what were you going to say about the boy at the Stuarts, the one in a wheelchair? I only saw a girl."

"Oh, I wondered . . . or it occurred to me, maybe the person we saw was a boy, not a girl."

Mid played scenes over in her mind. What she took as a deep alto could have been a lyric tenor. She remembered a school joke, changing the words of a popular song: *"I'm dancing with tears in my eyes / 'cause the girl in my arms is a boy."* Had she just assumed the figure she saw in the dark was a girl?

A girl in a wheelchair was not as tragic as a boy, though she couldn't say why. She recalled characters she'd encountered in Victorian novels, women become invalids after their childbearing years. They seemed oddly comfortable on sofas and reclining

67

couches, often the centers of attention at social gatherings. Younger and older men confessed their ambitions, courtship schemes, and political aspirations to them. And they were waited on by faithful servants.

Her own mother sometimes adopted a similar matriarchal role, resting while her children made sure beds were made, carpets cleaned, the laundry hung on the line. Mother would be reading poetry, writing letters, listening to the rest of the family talk of their day's events. Should Mid long for a life of action in remote places or such a position of privilege?

A German man had built an entire community to smelt iron--not just a furnace and a forge but a sawmill, a dam to create a larger water supply, roads and bridges to move the finished product. Were such adventures impossible for her?

The sound of music stopped. Mother must be talking to the Stuarts.

"Axel wouldn't want to have a picnic with those people," Ella said. "If he ever has a holiday, he uses it to study or work on his dad's equipment."

"Father loves to come here, but he never invites the people he works with," Mid observed. "They move in a different circle. Some have second homes on Long Island, not campsites."

No one in this family spoke about class. The fact that America had replicated an Old World social system they condemned was efficiently repressed. Mother could talk about proper behavior and Father could explain what it meant to be a gentleman in

68

business affairs. But that privilege was vested in family lines and that opportunities for advancement were controlled by vested interests were never acknowledged.

Years later, Mid would read about how this region was perfect for the iron industry: wide-ranging forests that provided fuel for the furnace; exposed ore that was easy to locate and extract; water descending from the hills that could be harnessed for power; and rivers providing transportation to markets. Still, the capital and experience of Europe were necessary to take advantage of a situation that the local population, raised in an agricultural environment, did not understand. The result for native and immigrant was a new, more prosperous way of life Just as the furnace fire, raised to more than 1500 degrees by giant bellows melted the magnetite to produce pig iron, so ancient social institutions refined skilled farm hands into pieces of an industrial machine, enriching all concerned.

Might the Stuart family own a plantation in Central or South America where one of their sons (the one able to walk, of course!) might take his great gifts--and a beloved--to forge a new way of life for the benefit of all mankind? More and more, Mid was becoming determined to take her place in the world's affairs, to be the subject of conversations, not the audience.

Chapter Ten: Charades

Sydney Stuart's kiss was pivotal in Mid's life. However, the summer at Greenwood Lake tended more to confirm an established trajectory in her life than to mark the dawning of a new world for her. Still, her understanding of that path was transformed.

The embrace occurred at Smelter's Point, the local spot famous for such encounters; and Mid connected her own experience to those of young lovers who had proposed and been accepted on this shore a hundred years before she entered the world. The picnic that provided the occasion was a surprise for her and her siblings, who never believed it would happen.

"They're coming?" Ella asked. "And Father agrees?"

At her mother's request, Mid had taken the ferry across to the landing so she could place the call. She had an hour's wait before Father rang back to say a summer picnic was fine. There was an echo on the line, his voice sounding as if it were traveling down a long canyon out West. Was he, by some chance, in Arizona or New Mexico? Maybe he was even farther away! In any case, the answer was yes--without explanation. They must have talked this over beforehand.

Still, Mid did not anticipate the Stuarts' prompt response. "I wrote them a very nice invitation," Mother explained. "It would have been rude to decline." Her daughters concluded that she had made Bill paddle her up there to deliver the note, not just speak to them.

What the Lacy children had failed to recognize was the reach of their mother's learning. It was not what Ethel said that appealed to her company, but the fact that she framed it within a literary context the other family understood. Indeed, they believed they lived in such imagined realms.

Gently poking fun at worn social rituals, Ethel invoked Elizabeth Barrett Browning's female poet, Aurora Leigh, who had insisted we should live in the present, *"this living, throbbing age, / That brawls, cheats, maddens, calculates, aspires, / And spends more passions, more heroic heat, / Betwixt the mirrors of its drawing-rooms, / Than Roland with his knights at Roncesvalles."*

Though he believed himself a descendant of chivalric heroes, Sydney wrote that they would "be pleased to attend." He used words from a Robert Browning poem to characterize the picnic site: *"Oh, good gigantic smile o' the brown old earth, / This autumn morning! How he sets his bones / To bask i' the sun, and thrusts out knees and feet / For the ripple to run over in its mirth . . . "* And the party as literary event was on.

Ethel put all the children to work making biscuits and potato salad, finding preserves, preparing fruit. They washed baskets and linen, cleaned dishes and silverware. She would bring a blanket to spread out on the rock, bottled drinks to keep cool in the lake, paper and pencil for her favorite game: charades.

While other families at this time were enthusiastic about a new version of the parlor game, in which clues were acted out, she held on to the more intellectual version, in which the answer had to be presented in poetic form: *"My first has just been born, / my second is worn late; / My whole's a part of union, / my being is a state."* New Jersey.

Mid was good at her mother's game and hoped it would turn Sydney's eyes toward her. She also knew the family beauty, Ella, would be absentminded, thinking of Ax and the prospect of Father's relenting. Although Alice's enthusiasm for play was engaging, surely the more sophisticated Stuarts would be impressed with learning, patience, reason.

Sydney pushed his brother, Bartholomew, in the bamboo wheelchair down the path to the point. His father and brother braced him on each side and helped him out onto the large stone outcrop at the water's edge. He'd had polio.

The Lacys knew about the epidemic of 1916 that began in Brooklyn, though this was before the two younger children came into the world. Father had always tried to keep the family away from places or people he believed were responsible for the spread of this and other diseases. He recounted dire tales of epidemics among poor populations in the Middle Ages.

Bart had been treated by foreign doctors, who avoided the wooden splints and plaster casts thought to minimize deformity. Massages and assisted exercise restored some ability to use his legs;

and he had a joyful approach to life that surprised Mid.

"I'm a musician," he told Mid. She had sat by him so as not to seem forward with his brother. The others were setting out the dishes. "I want to sing on the radio."

"Isn't it hard to get on those shows? Of course, I'm sure you're very good. We've heard you," she added, then blushed at how close she'd been, spying, really, on his family. "When the wind is right, it carries right down to our camp."

"Daddy will help me." He leaned closer to take an apple from the basket. "He knows Ben Bernie." After a pause, he added, "They wouldn't see me sitting, of course, and my voice would go from coast to coast."

"Maybe you can give us a song after we eat."

"Will you sing with me?"

"Alice will. She has a strong voice." Mid did not have a gift for music, though she loved to listen. "Excuse me. I must help Mother."

The woodland feast was a quiet success. It turned out that Father had business associates who knew the Stuart family. The bookkeeper of Curtis' insurance agency had gone to college with one of Moncrieff's financial advisors. And a company owned by the Stuart Trust insured its fleet of pleasure boats with his firm.

Bartholomew's mother was soft-spoken, an easy conversationalist who drew Bill out and shared child raising stories with Ethel. She talked about her seven years in Japan, daughter of a diplomat. She had met her husband in Yokahama, one stop on a cruise that took him to six continents.

Sydney politely asked Alice about her education, her music lessons, her interest in plants. Mid appreciated his social skills and hoped he would use them with her.

When the charades began, Mid prepared to step forward. Her insight and skill in language would draw him to her. Language would reach across the divides of background and experience, two like-minded individuals pulled close by literary allusions, word play, the fabric of culture. He would see in her abilities that were overlooked by her immediate family.

Or course, Mother was in her element, offering lyric clues and deciphering opaque descriptions that the other parents appreciated. Bart and Alice led everyone in laughter, even at their own wrong guesses. Ella, as if she had no other concerns on this mild summer day, threw herself into the game. And when "pilgrimage" was the subject, Bill had his moment of attention. But Mid felt the puzzles were all wrong for her. She played with less and less enthusiasm, wondering how she had fallen away from the group.

After a last round and before everyone prepared to depart, Ella, not Alice, joined Bart in an improvisational rendition of Bing Crosby's hit song, "Red Sails in the Sunset." She might, Mid reasoned, have been trying to keep from thinking about Axel and her future. From the edge of the woods, where she'd retreated, Mid saw their silhouettes against the water. A pretty picture and a pretty sound. Her sister's profile made her wonder if Sydney were looking at her. Where had he gone? She surveyed the scene.

Mid recalled Doctor Paterson's poem that had been preserved by her mother, the clue to another identity. Had Mid found it with this new family? Had the child struck by fever come back to the lake where she'd been taken to recover, ready now to move in a different social circle? Would she break out of the closeness of family to appear in distant places and different worlds? A kiss would confirm this change.

She saw them under the shadow of a giant oak: her sister Alice wrapped in Sydney's arms, limp beneath his kiss, lost to childhood forever. Mid was not the sweetheart.

Would she ever be? Or she was too balanced, too self-assured, too controlled to be swept away by a man? Everyone turned to her for resolution of problems, the easing of conflict, social comfort. Mid, who steered a middle course; Mid, who kept a level head; Mid, who was suspended between magnetic poles, pulled in all directions, but not one. The middle child.

That's where she'd be thirty years from now, she concluded. A maiden aunt, a parents' companion, the older woman who never found a husband but served others so well. Ella would marry Ax, Alice would run off with Sydney, Mid would take care of the parents.

Of course, she solved Sydney's difficult charade, though it gave her little satisfaction. "*My first is frost's near kin, / my second's me from birth ; / My last's the place I'm in; / but my whole goes off the earth.* Horizon." She could still hope Sydney was on her horizon, which, in fact, he was. Her true destiny, however, lay with another.

"That's all he did? He kissed you?"

Marian was deflated. The fictional account of her first romantic adventure on Greenwood Lake elicited this uninspiring response from Glenna. But her roommate at Archer was a far more experienced young woman even than the figure Mid pictured herself to have been. In fact, it was already Mid's plan to mimic Glenna's actions and attitudes in order to leave behind the girl who, she felt, had been jilted at Smelter's Point.

"The kiss was only the beginning." She smiled-- coyly, she hoped. "In the last week at the lake, we . . . we were like the bees in the buds and the birds in the forest."

"So, he deflowered you, a sweet young thing, and then flew away! And now you're worried that you're 'damaged goods' no medical student will be interested in. Oh, come on, Mild, only the devout churchgoers are virgins here." 'Mild' was her nickname for her reserved "Northern" roommate. She was from North Carolina. (And there were many virgins at this school.)

Mid was sitting on the black steamer trunk she'd brought with her on the train from Newark to Baltimore. The stickers from around the world were the result of her father's travel, but she let it be assumed she'd been to many of these remote places--

Bangkok, Venice, Buenos Aires. The closest she'd come to traveling to a foreign city was via the mail she exchanged infrequently with Tony, who was, she thought, somewhere near Barcelona in Spain.

"I've only met one medical student, and he was more interested in you." Mid had gone with Glenna to a party at Johns Hopkins that she thought would be attended by undergraduates like herself. But the smoky parlor was full of law students, interns, and post-graduates in the engineering program. She felt young and naive--which she was.

"Those would-be doctors are all the same--cheeky and eager." She laughed.

Glenna's chuckle was deep and gravelly, perhaps because she was a heavy smoker. The daughter of a well-known surgeon in Raleigh, she dismissed even Hopkins students as beneath her. True, she was an A student, always among the best in her science classes, though she claimed she'd never go into medicine like her father. He'd been away from his children too much--on rounds, at conferences, as a consultant--when they were growing up. Still, she didn't know what she wanted from life at this point, except to have fun.

"Well," Mid admitted, "I need to find some different sorts of boys. Or another way to amuse myself." There was one man--he seemed a boy--she remembered from the party. He had asked her if she'd read Marx.

Glenna repeated her invitation. "Come with me downtown. There's a great combo at the Long Wharf. You really can leave your knitting!" Nana's relentless instructions had paid off, and Mid always liked to have a project under way. This time it was a simple scarf.

"You're going to be out after curfew again, aren't you?"

Glenna gave her hoarse chuckle. On several Saturday nights she had stayed in their room until bed check, then slid open the window, lowered herself into the bushes, and boarded a bus to wherever she wanted to be. Mid couldn't bring herself to go along, especially after hearing what happened to one girl--and that in daylight. Taking this shortcut to the outside world was like time travel or riding on a flying carpet with Douglas Fairbanks as in *The Thief of Baghdad*.

Still, a vague restlessness made her want to break out. Father had chosen this school because it had a good academic reputation, and he felt she was the daughter who might make the most of study. That it was in Baltimore led him to conclude she would have no local contacts and thus devote herself to learning. Even her siblings wouldn't be able to visit, as she had when Ella was at Elmira. What Mid would do with this education had never been stated, but she assumed she should be a teacher--until she married, of course.

Still, looking back at the receding train platform from which her family waved goodbye, Mid had felt she was finally the one on the way to somewhere. If, at home, everyone had been too close for her to feel free, now she was hundreds of miles from being crowded in one house.

At Archer, she expected to be carried away by the teaching of a distinguished professor of English, an expert, perhaps, on the works of Dr. Paterson, her neighbor, who might have made a literary version of Marian immortal if she hadn't survived childhood illness. But in Miss Bach's course Mid found herself diagramming sentences and parsing medieval texts until she came to believe she hated language itself. 'Westward, Ho,' she said, declaring she would major in history.

The predictions she sent home in letters featured Mid enlightening Rutherford school children about how America became a destination for the world's poor: the "*huddled masses yearning to breathe free, / The wretched refuse of your teeming shore. / Send these, the homeless, tempest-tossed to me* . . . " The private horoscope she hoped to read, however, might have said, "You will receive a letter soon that takes you to another Continent."

When she did receive an invitation--to travel halfway across this Continent--she accepted quickly. Father had to see some clients in St. Louis and suggested, because it would come in January, between terms, that she take the train out with him. It was still several months off, but it would carry Mid farther from home than she'd ever been.

Young Dr. Fahr had already made the land west of the Mississippi enticing. Of course, many students found *him* enticing. And he knew how to encourage their adoration.

"Miss Lacy," he might ask in class, "If I requested you to accompany me to Andorra, what should you carry to ensure our comfort?" She imagined him on a snow-covered mountaintop, surveying the lands to the south for hidden troops who aimed to expand Nationalist territory at the expense of France. Then she saw herself serving him steaming coffee, a touch of brandy added, when he returned to headquarters, warning of attack.

"You would want winter clothes, of course. The atmosphere is thin at those elevations."

"Quite so, Ms. Lacy." Then she imagined him adding, "Drop by my office this evening to talk more about the fragile boundaries between countries and people. Better yet, let's have tea this afternoon at a quaint cafe I've found in Fells Point."

Dr. Fahr's speciality was early American history, and he lectured enthusiastically about European immigrants, westward expansion, the establishment of a new nation. The frontier drew him on like a wearied sea traveler's beacon glimpsed far off in a storm. Marian caught his passion and imagined herself as an intrepid individual carving destiny out of the wilderness somewhere beyond the Great Plains.

Describing wagon trains headed down the Santa Fe Trail, Dr. Fahr compared those pioneers to the present day Okies fleeing failed farms in the Depression. He talked about Route 66, the path of migration to fresh starts in California, but acknowledged many families settled in make-shift new communities on the edges of existing towns-- Hoovervilles. Still, he made all these journeys seem exotic, as if anyone who embarked on such a pilgrimage would be fulfilled.

So, if Mid wasn't to be seduced by her history professor (as, some said, Tricia Neigh had already been) or courted by a medical student (as Glenna could be), she kept her hopes alive that a stranger would get off a restored steamboat cruising icy, mid-winter Old Man River and show her the joys of gambling. (Later she would be convinced that something very much like that had happened.) In the meantime, she thought, slipping off her steamer trunk to sit at her desk, there was first-year German to study.

"You know who might be at the Long Wharf?" Glenna asked. "Sydney's brother. I've heard of him. And if he's singing, wouldn't his family be there to add to the audience?"

Mid had left wheelchairs out of her account of summer romance. It wasn't, she thought, essential to the supposed tryst between the New England aristocrat and the young maiden. She'd been haunted in some ways by the image of a man unable to go up stairs, to run through the woods, to ice skate on a lake. Bart's lack of mobility was like the restrictions she believed she faced herself, only worse: his own body created them.

On the other hand, her body was also a source of limitation: being a woman meant she could not be a missionary on her own, as Bill would be soon; nor could she expect to rise in business or a profession, as her older brother would after he completed his degree this year.

"Sydney . . . I told Sydney I wouldn't see him again. I . . .. I couldn't."

Glenna sat up on the edge of the bed. "Why not?"

"Because I . . . even though he's ever so rich and so talented that . . . well, I have my own ideas about what I'm going to do, where I'll go."

"You haven't told me about them."

It was true that Mid kept her plans to herself: first, because she was reticent about confiding in her outspoken, assertive roommate; and second, of course, because she was also making up her schemes at that very moment.

"After this year," she insisted, "I'm going abroad, as a governess."

Chapter Twelve: Lost

Marian had read *Mary Lavelle*, Kate O'Brien's novel about a woman who became a governess in Spain after university. The book suggested the author had radical social tendencies, but Mid responded mostly to the adventurous heroine. And when backed into a corner by Glenna, she took the heroine out of this book as a temporary model for herself.

In Rutherford she'd found herself constantly likened either to Ella or Alice, as if she were a version of one of them. She learned that association could mean definition. With her older sister now married and living in Maine, her younger sister still in high school back home, she was certain she could finally be understood on her own terms. Sadly, she wasn't sure what her own terms were!

The idea of attaching herself to a wealthy family-- that would surely come to treat her more like a daughter than a servant--did have its appeal. She also at times imagined herself as secretary to an important financial figure visiting branch offices in Ohio or Missouri or California. The local bank president, surprisingly young, would fall for her and she'd end up raising a family in Cleveland or St. Louis, or San Francisco.

However, she had more immediate concerns. For one, she needed to get a new lab partner.

Diana Tracy had latched onto Mid the first day of physiology class. This shy West Virginian's inability to retain even the most basic instructions (how to measure the length of a cat's intestine) had made Mid fear Professor Royal would conclude neither women at that table worth her attention. Mid had already had to divert students at neighboring lab tables from registering Diana's obtuseness. She wasn't sure she could do that with the instructor.

Dr. Royal had been hired by the most famous female professor at Archer, Dr. Schure, and was transforming what had been the study of personal hygiene into a laboratory science. This was a new field in which women were beginning to work, publish, and prosper--though not, of course, at the same rate as men who entered medical school. Mid didn't think she'd major in science, but her professor's stories about treating war invalids in England made her see a potential for travel as part of the discipline. Still, if work at a medical lab were in her future, she'd have to separate herself from Diana, who was slow to learn and had been branded in some ways for what happened when she went off campus back in September.

Mid also had a second problem perhaps as urgent: she had received a letter from Sydney Stuart just this morning from Rhode Island, the family home. He didn't explain how he knew where she was, or make any reference to her sister. He was offering to take her to the matinee performance of *Lost Horizons* at the Hippodrome on Saturday. Mid hovered between accepting out of curiosity and throwing the letter away out of resentment.

When Glenna did disappear later that evening, Mid was still at her desk with an unstudied German textbook open in front of her: "*Ich werde an Preußen. Wo willst du hin?*" She opened Sydney's letter and read it again: " . . . will happen to be in town;" "thought you might like to see . . . ;" " . . . renew our Greenwood Lake connection." He'd given her the address of the hotel where he'd be staying; and she still had a day to decide.

She'd read Thomas Hilton's famous book about a valley hidden high in the Himalayas whose residents possessed wisdom and never aged. The play would be a means of travel, she concluded, at least in her imagination. Via the power of theater, she would have the chance to leave Baltimore and experience a vastly different world: she'd be at a high altitude instead of sea level; she'd feel cold in mountain air compared to comfortable in the Indian summer that had made Glenna's leaving the window open appropriate; and she'd have a view that would be Eastern and mystical as opposed to Western and scientific.

Having seen other campuses (Columbia University, for instance), the only strange world she'd seen since leaving Rutherford was the microscopic one in Dr. Royal's laboratory. There, rather than the tiny creatures that lived in pond water she'd viewed in her high school science class, Mid watched unknown creatures swimming in her own saliva. An inside view of the self, she'd thought, as she tried to help Diana focus her instrument.

She took a piece of the embossed note paper her father had given her and settled herself to write--first to her sister, Alice; then--when she'd decided what to say--to Sydney.

Reading and writing letters from home was like looking through a telescope: she could see the house on Ridge Road where, at Sunday dinner, Nana fretted about the *Nationalsozialistische Deutsche Arbeiterpartei*'s solidification of power and Grandpa still imagined himself putting in turnips and winter squash on his upstate farm. She was drawn toward the comfortable scene but at the same time yearned for a different style--a cultured life, perhaps, in which, elegantly dressed, she might go to the opera, then to a late dinner party with titled men and women.

Before she put the first word down tonight, however, she was interrupted by a knock on the door: her sad lab partner had come for help in understanding the circulatory system of a rat.

"It's all right there in our book," Mid told her, pointing to her own copy on the shelf above her desk. "Look at the diagrams." She was studying Diana's troubled face, which reminded her vaguely of Bill's after his near drowning in Greenwood Lake.

"But there are so many parts--the brachiocephalic artery, right subclavian artery, the left common carotid artery. All those atriums and cavas. I can't keep them straight."

"'Atrium' is another word for room. Think of the heart as a house with many rooms. And the blood is like the heat from your furnace, flowing through all the ducts and cold air returns."

"We only have wood stoves, one in each room. Besides . . . besides . . . "

"What is it?" Mid sensed tears were about to well up in Diana's eyes, and her own voice became more tender. She gestured toward the bed. "Sit. Take some deep breaths. There's more to this than a rodent's heart, isn't there?"

Diana gave a little sob and buried her face in her hands. But she got herself under control. "Why is Dr. Royal mad at me? She wants me to come by her office."

"Is she . . . maybe she plans to give you extra tutoring. She probably just wants you to pass the course. She wants us all to do well."

"No, it's not that. It happened after that day I was late."

Mid remembered: Diana had forgotten her lab report, realized it just before class was to begin, and raced across campus to get it.

"But you got back quickly. I didn't think Dr. Royal even noticed." Mid had been able to watch her partner through the classroom window running across the quadrangle. She didn't stop, had to go up to three flights in her dormitory, and came flying back. When she slipped in the back and sat down beside Mid, she hadn't seemed winded at all. Mid thought Dr. Royal might not have been aware of what had happened.

"I hoped she wouldn't notice. But she called me up after class. I . . . I had to confess about the report. But, you know, Mid, she didn't seem upset. She kind of smiled and said everything was fine. But if that's true, why would she want me to report to her office? And why did she want to know the schedule of all my classes? Why did she ask about my home, what my parents do?"

Mid couldn't answer her questions. She knew Diana was the first in her family to go to college and wanted desperately to succeed, so Mid got her textbook out and worked with her for an hour, pointing to the arrows that traced blood flow, explaining the diagram of the hepatic portal system, reviewing the ways in which oxygen is carried to tissue and toxins are removed.

Mid was puzzled. She wanted Dr. Royal's attention herself and had even gone by her office to explain how much she was enjoying the class. The professor was polite but did not prolong the discussion. What did she see in Diana? Once again, Mid seemed to be eclipsed by someone else, not a sister this time but another student--and one of obviously lesser ability.

She re-read the most recent letter from Alice, who felt abandoned this fall. Since Ella had eloped with Axel and Mid had gone off to college, the youngest daughter had no one her age to confide in. Her closest sibling, Bill, was caught up in his missionary fever, and, as far as Mid knew, there had been no correspondence from Sydney. So Alice wrote long, lonely letters to her sisters. Mid had the inclination and more time to write than Ella, a young wife trying to bring in extra money by sewing and repairing worn garments.

Alice's correspondence chronicled Curtis and Ethel's gradual movement toward reconciliation with Ella and forgiveness of Axel, who was succeeding in his new position. An unspoken fear was that Ella would become pregnant. People were still having a hard time in the Depression, and if there were one more family member to feed--an aging parent or a newborn--bankruptcy threatened. Still, Ella had at least gotten away from Rutherford.

Mid wrote to Sydney that she'd be happy to accompany him to *Lost Horizons*.

Chapter Thirteen: Bridges

Timothy Jensen brought her a copy of *Das Kapital*.

"That's so very nice," she said. "How . . . thoughtful." She had only a vague idea of what this book was about, but she knew from her father that Marx was dangerous.

She and her guest were in "The Gather," a recent innovation at Archer, which, until the last year, had not allowed smoking anywhere on campus. Mid hoped it would not be said she had invited Tim to add to the smoke-filled atmosphere. In the middle of a bridge game, she had been as surprised as anyone when the house mother told her she had a visitor.

Other new aspects of Archer residence hall life at the time included less stringent chapel attendance (you were supposed to go, but roll was not taken) and "weekend permissions" for those students whose parents authorized them. Change, apparently, was in the air.

"If you want to know what's going on," Tim added, "in places like Russia and Germany, you need to read this."

Mid was wondering why in the world he had sought her out. At the Hopkins party, she'd had no more conversation with him than with half a dozen other young men. She couldn't even remember what they'd talked about, and, self-conscious, didn't see how she'd make an impression on him. Still, to be polite, she asked, "Are you studying government?"

"History. I want to be a professor and study abroad. There's so much to be done, and this country only thinks about making money."

"Ah. I'll probably be a history teacher myself, back home in New Jersey."

She looked around The Gather, perhaps for inspiration on how to end this conversation. Timothy, long and lean, looked as if he needed gathering himself. His clothes were wrinkled and a bit worn; his dark hair, parted in the middle, was shaggy around the ears; his long limbs seemed to have independent sections that could assemble themselves at odd angles. Still, he had an odd intensity that intrigued Mid when he peered down at her from his high vantage point.

He leaned down closer now. "So, do you want to be part of the international struggle?"

"The . . . struggle? I'm not sure I understand."

"We have to unite with the workers, like you said."

"I said . . . ?" She tried to replay their conversation at the party. Had she mentioned that her father was a successful businessman? That would hardly have encouraged Tim's question. Did she appear so conspicuously bourgeois that he felt a need to convert her? Only if she'd talked about a desire to travel might she have suggested an interest in "international" matters.

Fortunately, he went on. "The cafeteria workers, the grounds people, the janitors and maintenance crews. The Negroes can't attend classes, but they're really just like you and me. We're at the same level, brothers and sisters who make up the masses. And we need to reach across the artificial social barriers that divide us."

Then it came back to her: she'd helped an old Negro woman who was emptying ash trays, picking up empty glasses, carrying away trays of food. One of the law students wanted "Miss Milly" to move furniture so they could dance, but she didn't understand what he was asking. Mid instinctively volunteered, and Tim had stepped in to push back a sofa. It would be many years before she learned that the language connecting master to servant was governed by strict codes. While an employer could give any order, if it had no precedent in a worker's experience, it would mean nothing when it reached the employee's ears.

"Well, yes. I sometimes feel sorry for them . . . but they have different lives. They have their own schools."

She really hadn't thought about it. Segregation in the North was de facto. When she saw signs for "Colored" in the South, it seemed simply to spell out an element of the system she was familiar with and accepted. A member of that race would no more want to attend Archer than she desired to enroll at . . . whatever schools there were for Negroes.

Her father's opinion about the working classes, white or black, was benevolent, assuming that bosses took care of employees through responsible management. The workers would have chances to rise, though few had the natural ability or the resourcefulness to move up the social ladder. Immigrants from Europe, like Axel's family, might make that transition, but slowly over several generations. The separation of classes was natural and unchangeable.

"We're having a meeting next week at The Maryland Coffee House. Do you know where that is?"

She had no idea. And she did not want to find herself with some revolutionary group intent on inciting revolution.

"I . . . um . . . have to study for my physiology exam. And I have a composition due, but why don't I send you a note if I'm free. Or call." Then she added, "Well, I also have this book to read." She smiled and held up *Das Kapital*.

She could see he was disappointed, but he didn't seem angry. "It's in Federal Hill. I can come get you, if . . . if you find you have time." They left it at that.

When she thought about it later, Mid confirmed to herself that she was hardly a rebel. Like the Stuarts, the Lacys came from a branch of old aristocracy, or at least an ancient English family. In fact, Mid could think of herself as having inherited an Old World understanding brought by her ancestors to Nantucket, one of the first European settlements in North America. Wouldn't she be more of a match for someone like Sydney than Tim?

After the bridge game, she was angry at herself for thinking again that her identity had to be shaped by the man she was with. She imagined herself in one of the scenes Dr. Royal had described from her

94

time in Europe, nurses and other female medical personnel unwinding at the end of a long work day by playing cards.

Evenings were long in the English summer, and the extended twilight made Mid's professor, then just out of school and out of the country for the first time, feel as if she'd entered a different world. The men she had worked with were forgotten, but not all her patients.

Dr. Royal had recalled a man who had suffered multiple injuries when a shell landed in his battlefield trench. In the course of the regular early morning bombardment, he'd been compacting himself, he hoped, to microscopic littleness. But he had not been missed.

Donald Miles told the then young Penelope Royal that he was a church organist. He was depressed, he said, not so much by the horror of what he'd experienced, but the impact it would have on his musical career. Broken bones in both legs and one arm were going to restrict the reach he had possessed from his late teen years. He was sure he wouldn't be able to extend his feet to hit pedals cleanly, and limited mobility in his left shoulder put the lowest base notes out of reach. Penelope told him he could adjust with practice.

"It's like music itself is out of reach, though," he replied sadly. "Or I'm in somebody else's body, someone who might have played a spinet."

Corporal Miles was in his cane wheelchair. He could walk with braces and a cane, but only for short distances. They told him it would be some time before he was strong enough to be on his own. But there was something else the doctors were aware of, something he couldn't understand.

"The war has changed us all," Penelope explained to him gently. "I was engaged to a man who was going to law school. When he came back, he couldn't keep away from drink. My family finally had to call the wedding off."

This was true, but not the whole story. Penelope's experience while he was overseas convinced her she could do well in a medical field on her own. She had answered the national call to help those who promised to "make the world safe for democracy." When she returned, she found herself being aggressively recruited by several local hospitals. And, in the end, she came to understand that women might have as many opportunities as men in a post-war world.

"I bet your fiancé still could practice law," Donald insisted. His hands played over an imaginary keyboard on the folded blanket. She wondered what tune he thought he was playing.

The convalescent hospital had contacted Miles' family. When they came to visit, Penelope learned he'd never been a musician at all. The fantasy must have come from a book he'd read or perhaps a fellow soldier's battlefield story. He hadn't been in his right mind since the shell landed--or, quite possibly, well before that horrific culmination of his last battle.

While the boy's fingers drumming on the blanket haunted Penelope, the picture Mid retained from that story was of the women working together far from home. And she saw herself doubling and redoubling outrageous bids in future bridge games, happy to be beyond the reach of convention.

Chapter Fourteen: Bids

Mid felt herself out of the reach of convention whenever Glenna was her bridge partner.

She could use Blackwood, Gerber, or Ingbergman, but when her roommate glared at her, telepathy would have to be the only system by which she could understand her partner.

Still, Mid had learned this game more quickly than others at Archer and felt privileged when her roommate wanted her on the other side of the table, even if she was more often the dummy than the declarer. She was less adventurous than Glenna, of course, but counted points quickly, remembered what had been played, and balanced gain against risk as if she'd played much longer than she had. The night before she was to see *Lost Horizons*, Mid had surprised the other players by bidding a grand slam.

Her family were eager game players, as the Stuarts learned when Ethel was the host for charades at the Lake. Grandfather reigned as the house's champion checkers player; Grandma scheduled a round robin cribbage tournament each year from Christmas to New Year's; and the children had marathon Canasta sessions on rainy summer days at the lake.

Bridge at Archer, though, added an element to recreation that was new to Mid: a competitiveness that lingered and spread. It was unsettling but also curiously exhilarating. Whatever the reasons behind such intensity, play in this environment was significantly distanced from the innocent and simpler games she'd played with her siblings.

"You're sure?" Glenna questioned, holding her cards at Mid's final bid.

"Double," said Margot, the flute player from Scranton.

Glenna smiled, "Redouble," and spread out her cards for Mid to see.

She was not at all sure she could make it, but she was angry that June had earlier suggested Glenna could make more of the hands Mid was dealt. Losing would only confirm this negative opinion of her, but winning might be an event remembered from the evening.

Decades later she would conclude that the times affected everything they did at college. Even leisure was tinged with an awareness of trouble soon to come. Signs of impending war were regularly heard from Europe, and the economic struggle at home grew more desperate, to the point that even the privileged felt almost constant apprehension.

The older generation hoped the United States could stay out of conflicts they had no clear stake in, even if they understood that the country's future was tied to the world's business. When they were supposed to be busy elsewhere, children picked up on the tone of anxiety in hushed adult conversations. Young men at college wondered if their degrees would matter in the slaughter recalled by and predicted by veterans of the Great War.

Older women like Penelope Royal, who'd already seen great changes in how women behaved after WWI, saw opportunity in the future, so long as the country survived. But Mid's fellow students, most quite comfortable within the traditional framework of "Normal" schools for women, sensed threats that lay just off the campus. And such awareness generated tensions in unconnected activities, even play.

"You'd better make this," Glenna said grimly.

Ah, her partner had the necessary queen of spades, thought Mid. Now if the finesse only worked! She was gambling that June would hold the ace for one round if she led from the board. Mid had no protection for her singleton king.

When Mid agreed to let Sydney take her to *Lost Horizons*, she was accepting without thought his masculine protection, an extension, really, of the authority of senior officers who ran Archer. She would not confront the danger less privileged girls like Diana had.

On the first weekend of the school year, the girl who would soon be Mid's lab partner, had wanted to see the harbor; bays and oceans had only been read about on her West Virginia farm. She didn't fully take in all the college regulations about signing out, traveling in groups, having your itinerary approved. She saw Baltimore as a flatter farm than her Daddy's 100 acres and more marked by buildings. Surely she could walk tree-lined streets and parks on her own in broad daylight?

The man who asked if she were by herself had seemed friendly, feeding pigeons from a bench on Light Street. Perhaps she assumed, because the birds were unafraid, like her chickens back home, that he represented no danger. Her attention was directed mostly to the gigantic steamboats loading passengers for weekend trips to amusement parks on the Eastern Shore. She also watched a string of cargo ships bringing in oysters and produce from local farms.

Mid knew the scene herself from later, college sanctioned excursions. On her first visit she gazed past the piers and boats to their destinations, manifest in ships' names--*The City of Norfolk, City of Havre, City of Hamburg*. Did such descendants of the famous Baltimore Clippers now carry the Stuarts to the far corners of the globe? Had Sydney started out on a journey toward Shangri La from such a place? Would there be a berth for her on a ship currently steaming away from America toward, say, Hong Kong or Melbourne, Australia?

The feeder of pigeons was inching toward Diana on the bench he had offered to share. Smelling the salt air and hearing a bustling city life, she didn't really take in his chatter.

"I owned two warehouses here once." He waved his hand vaguely behind him. "We shipped manufactured goods from factories around the state to Africa and the Orient. There were rooms full of mattresses, crates of syrup, clothes. And companies begged for space to store their goods before transport."

Watching a ship unloading melons, Diana must have been thinking about the farms across the water, rich flat land that made it a canning center for tomatoes and fruits. Her father had read about the good soil over there, so much easier to work than the rocky and hilly ground the family owned. And the weather near the ocean was kinder to plants and animals.

Diana never told Mid the details of her encounter, but a version grew in Mid's mind that was so full of detail and so consistent in tone that she began to believe it was the truth. Other accounts circulated around campus, even one that came out of the Dean's office and was intended as a lesson to all new students. But Mid held to the story she told Ella when she was home at Christmas. Once presented there, it was history.

As Diana watched trucks being loaded with crates of beets, lima beans, and gourds, the former warehouse owner was sliding along the bench closer and closer to her side. "Sure, I was a big shot for a while there, but then came the Crash. My bank closed, and I couldn't get to my money. Suppliers couldn't pay to transport goods to the city. Overseas markets dried up. Here I was, owner of huge empty buildings."

Diana got up to go. Homesick for her West Virginia family, she hadn't really been listening. The man rose with her and grabbed her arm. "Don't go now, missy. You'll want to see my old office. It's just down here. There's a side door in the alley."

While he was thin and probably hungry, the man was strong and believed he could pull Diana with him. He may have done it to another girl before, and he assumed that this one, too, would be so frightened he could overpower her.

But rather than pull away in an attempt to run, Diana stepped toward him, holding onto his wrist with the hand he had attempted to grip. She brought her knee up so forcefully and accurately that the man blacked out for a moment as he doubled over and fell forward. Her fingers were still tightly closed on his arm as she watched him go down, deciding it was not necessary to kick him to make him stay there. Diana had wrestled her older brothers in play and dealt with some aggressive schoolmates on her own.

She reported the incident to Miss Wrenn, the dorm mother, not because she had been worried about her welfare but because she thought men like that should be put to work by the government so that they wouldn't be out on the streets. Ms. Dupont, the Dean of Students, who had herself once similarly thwarted a man's attack, chuckled at the frank account she received.

Mid got June's ace on the second spades trick. Running out trump, she had only one other pitfall to manage: she would have to count on Margot's at some point discarding the seven of clubs, as her last lead would be the six. Watching the cards being thrown by her opponents gave her an icy thrill. She took in each trick as if she was completely confident she had winners in every suit now. It was a matter of simply playing it out.

Of course, had June been less surprised at Mid's bold bid and her apparent confidence, she might have realized that, if the declarer been absolutely sure, she would have laid down her cards. Only when the six of clubs appeared did she realize, too late, she could have stopped the doubled and redoubled bid.

Chapter Fifteen: Travelers

Mid had never sat so close to a stage, even when her high school put on *Strike Up the Band*, and she came early because John would be singing "I've Got a Crush on You." The box Sydney had reserved for *Lost Horizons* was on the left side of the theater and barely higher than the actors' heads. When the curtains parted for the first scene, she felt she could have stepped over the rail into the dining room of the British embassy in Berlin, where the manuscript of Robert Conway was being read.

Before that, of course, she was self-consciously aware of where she was in reality--very much in Sydney's presence. Beside him in the taxi, she had smelled his cologne, felt the shoulder of his fine suit sometimes touch the jacket she had borrowed from Glenna, worried that he was able to scrutinize her hair, her complexion, the color (brown with gold flecks) of her eyes.

Later she also realized, sitting so far up front, that the rest of the theater audience could inspect her as long as the lights were up. Sydney had offered her the seat closest to the stage, so he was partially hidden by her. Because the box matching theirs on the other side of the theater was empty, she and Sydney were the most prominent spectators of the night. To some in the balcony, then, it might have appeared that she *was* in the play!

"I was surprised to learn you were in school here," he observed after they were seated. On the way, they'd both given accounts of their various family members. She waited nervously for him to make an inquiry about Alice, but he did not, apparently satisfied with the simple statement that she was doing fine at Rutherford High. She and Alice had never discussed what happened at the picnic.

"You were surprised that I was here?" she asked.

"Well, I thought you would stay in the area, perhaps The New Jersey College for Women?"

"Father thought it would be good for me to be more on my own. Archer does have a good reputation."

Sydney put two fingers to the spot where the brim of his hat would be if it were on, and Mid assumed he must have seen someone he knew over her shoulder. Being careful not to turn around and look, she wondered if any of her classmates would be in the audience. And would they see her, maker of grand slam bridge contracts and guest of an elegant man of the world?

"We've put up here on our way south," Sydney said. "It's a nice little town."

"'Put up'?"

"Our yacht. We harbor at our house in the Keys for the summer. There are regular trips to the Bermuda estate . . . to make sure all is well there."

She tried to imagine the boat, a second home in Florida, the Caribbean property that . . . what? . . . produced income (sugar?) or served as a family resort?

"You have marine insurance, then, with Father's company?"

"We do now, and we also refer firms we work with to him. His is a good company. But you know that." He smiled gently.

The play began, and, in her mind's eye, snowy Himalayas replaced the Stuarts' tropical estates. At less eventful moments in the drama, however, her thoughts strayed back to the present. She wondered why her escort had picked her up in a mere taxi. Didn't he have limousines in every city (as well, probably, as a girl in each port)? Why was this man escorting her, a college student who'd grown up in a quiet suburban neighborhood with middle and working class neighbors, a woman who occasionally rode the bus into Manhattan to window shop for dresses she couldn't afford, and someone who only read about countries she hoped to see one day? He was as alien to her sphere as Conway was to the serene residents of Shangri La.

At the intermission Mid insisted on stretching her legs, though Sydney offered to bring her anything she wanted from the refreshment bar. "Of course," he smiled, "if you need the Powder Room . . . ," and moved aside so she could step out of the box. What she really wanted to do was mingle with the other theater goers, speculate about their station in life, consider if she belonged with people who dreamed of Utopia.

In Rutherford she and her siblings had loved going to the movies. They whispered through the news reel footage, laughed at the cartoons, and thrilled at the cliff-hanging episodes of the weekly serials. For Mid every feature was an avenue to romance. The well-dressed and subdued strangers she saw around her tonight, however, contrasted with the Empire's boisterous crowd.

One young man did remind her of moviegoers she might see back home. He was thin and somewhat bent over, as if recovering from illness or injury. And, looking directly at her, his eyes burned against shaggy hair and a full beard, reminding her of Tim Jensen, the ardent socialist.

Turning away from the unsettling face, she asked Sydney, "I suppose you attend plays on Broadway regularly?"

"When I'm in town, yes. Providence has Lowe's. My brother has sung there."

"I understand he's appearing at the Long Wharf?"

"Ah, yes. It's rather late, of course." He looked down at his shoes, as if apologizing that he had not invited her there also. Archer would not have allowed it, of course.

She wondered if Bart would have been happy to see her in his audience. She'd spent more time with him during the picnic at Greenwood Lake than with his older brother, who'd ended up kissing Alice in a scene that had fixed itself in Mid's memory.

She had not let on that she witnessed that embrace, and, apparently, she had been the only one who had, other than the participants. Mid's initial anger had been muted by shame at her hubris--as if he would want the middle sister! Alice never referred to the kiss or to Sydney. Once back in Rutherford, she'd become a quiet high school student once again. Even though her letters now were confessional in tone, Mid would learn what she was really thinking months later.

Mid looked back to see Sydney stopping to speak with an older woman--well, older than she was, though probably not yet thirty. She was poised and attractive. Sydney saw Mid raising her eyebrows and held up a finger to suggest he would only be a minute. She went on toward their box, carrying with her a mental picture of an elegantly dressed, sophisticated woman.

Was this his girl in this port? Was it inevitable that, wherever Sydney went in society, there would be . . . what, a distant cousin, the fiancée of a business associate, some former debutante from Providence's elite women's clubs who would show up Mid as . . . as . . . plain, balanced, ordinary. Mid, who steered a middle course; Mid, who kept a level head; Mid, who was suspended between magnetic poles, pulled in all directions, but not one.

Glenna, who seemed to know everything, had told her the upper classes of Providence were a backward lot, reluctant to accept into their organizations successful members of a growing immigrant population. Newcomers from Germany, Italy, eastern Europe had been necessary to the industrial prosperity of the area, but the more established aristocratic families resented their increasing political power. How did Sydney fit in that social ordering?

The Lacys--at least her father--tended to be apolitical, a product in part of the Quaker tradition of their ancestors. Coming to Baltimore, a "Southern" city, had made Mid think outside the framework of her family.

Before she had a chance to find out about the woman Sydney had met or his associates in Rhode Island, the play resumed. Mid lost herself in the scene where Robert Conway is asked to become the spiritual leader of the unique religious community in Tibet. At the same time, another member of his party, Mallinson is preparing to leave the monastery with the beautiful and exotic Lo-tsen. He convinces Conway to help him down the mountain.

A curtain at the back of the stage representing the High Lama's chamber wall is pulled back for the next scene, revealing a dazzling panoramic of the mountains drawn on canvas. A narrow path winds down, down, down to a final, barely visible turning.

"Don't go," Mid finds herself telling Conway in her imagination. "Around that last bend of the trail is what you've known all your life, a conventional existence. Even if you don't share all of the High Lama's beliefs, you have a chance to discover secrets of the ages."

Then she thinks about Lo-tsen, who is leaving what for her is the familiar. She will descend to the unknown, a world she has experienced only through rumor and conjecture. While the play centers on Conway and his manuscript, Mid's mind remains fixed on the Chinese woman who ventures into, not away from, "civilization."

110

On her way through the lobby, still slightly giddy from the fantasy, Mid was startled by the haunted face she had seen earlier. The man stepped in front of her. When she stiffened, Sydney pulled her away from the stranger by her elbow.

"Marian," the man said. "Don't you recognize me? It's Tony Giordano, from Rutherford."

Chapter Sixteen: Subjects

She did not speak at length with her childhood neighbor--once her would-be sweetheart--for several days. Startled at his appearance in the theater lobby, she couldn't sustain a conversation. Sydney, sensing her confusion, had been politely protective.

Tony had known Mid was at Archer, but not that she would be in the audience of *Lost Horizons*. Of course, he had spotted her in the box up front and confronted her more on impulse than with deliberation.

He might have been the last person she expected to meet at a play in Baltimore, Maryland. As far as she knew, he'd been in Spain for more than a year. Directly in front of her, though, he looked ghastly.

Sydney gently interposed himself between Mid and Tony. "Perhaps this isn't the best place for you two New Jersey natives to talk. Marian?" And it was quickly agreed that Tony would telephone her Sunday afternoon and make arrangements to come to Archer one evening, when they would have time to talk.

He had taken the bus up for the day from Fort Meade, where he'd been for several weeks. Mid could not imagine what had happened to him, or figure out why he so earnestly wanted to speak with her. Surely she had been clear that she didn't want to marry him. And hadn't he committed himself to the cause in Spain, whatever exactly that cause was?

Before she could learn more about the former boy next door, Sydney ushered her into a taxi, and she was taken back to her dormitory. At this hour, Sydney could go no farther than the foyer to watch her sign in and release him from responsibility for her. There she said goodbye to her escort of the night, but it might, she came to realize, have been more a farewell. He explained that he would be on a train headed to Memphis (via the nation's capital) in the morning.

"Business?"

"Yes. And some pleasure. I'll be the guest of an old friend from Brown. He inherited a plantation up near Sikeston, Missouri, along the Mississippi." Sydney laughed softly. "He's learning to grow cotton, a Quaker from Pennsylvania! Apparently, they're having a bit of trouble with . . . ah, the natives." Mid didn't want to know what kind of trouble he meant--or what he meant by the term, "natives"--so she thanked him for a "delightful evening" (Glenna had told her to be sure to use the phrase) and retreated into the dorm.

Much later, when she lived in Missouri herself and came to feel almost a native, she learned what "trouble" came to the Bootheel, though her life in the center of the state would be safe from that particular turmoil.

It was, in the end, a strange night. Sydney had not suggested he might see her in the future, even at their neighboring properties along Greenwood Lake. He'd asked little about Alice. It seemed as if he simply wanted a way to pass an evening while on his own in Baltimore. He had hardly strained his intellect or his charm all evening.

She thought of her brother singing "I've Got a Crush on You" in high school and concluded Sydney had no crush on her, or, for that matter, on Alice. In *Strike Up the Band,* high chocolate tariffs lead the United States and Switzerland into war, despite the fact the two countries share many values. In *Lost Horizons,* the conflict was philosophical or religious, two cultures separated by an enormous chasm. Between Mid and Sydney there had been neither closeness nor distance, friction nor friendship, understanding nor questions.

A deepening involvement with her lab partner, however, resumed that very evening, pushing Stuarts and Giodanos to the back of her mind for the next few days. Moments after Mid reached her room, Diana rushed in the open door and plumped down on the bed next to her.

"Dr. Royal called me into her office again," she told Mid excitedly. "She wants me to participate in an experiment. I'm to be a 'subject.'" She was beaming, and Mid backed up a little on the bed, worried that she was about to be embraced.

Formal contact, like the handshake, had its place in the Lacy, Puritan ethic of simplicity and reserve, but there was little hugging in Mid's family. She tried to keep Diana where she was with a question, "You'll be tested?"

Mid was guessing Diana would be part of a study for the college, perhaps to find out whether certain schools prepared their students sufficiently for the

114

Archer curriculum. Her own performance so far--a consistent B student--showed that Rutherford had done well.

"Yes, and she wants to talk to you, too."

Now, this was promising. Mid had wanted to be recognized by this engaging professor.

She looked closely at Diana, who seemed more animated and confident than she had been all semester (unless, of course, you count the time that failed businessman in downtown Baltimore thought he could take advantage of an innocent, country girl).

"What are we going to do? Tell me all about it."

As she spoke, though, Mid pulled her legs up on the bed and wrapped her arms around them, forcing Diana to settle down at the other end of the bed.

"Well," Diana looked away. "I think we'll do different things. I'm supposed to . . . um . . . do actions, like throw the medicine ball and, ah, go up and down stairs. Me and two other girls."

Mid considered herself a fit specimen, always loving to walk and skate and swim. But her job might be to observe others, perhaps in some sort of behavioral psychology study. Maybe the physical exercise was meant to improve self-confidence. Mid would be a coach or a tutor, as well as a scientific observer. She imagined herself with a bound journal for record keeping, a pile of books on health and medical treatment, perhaps space in one of the physiology laboratories to write up her findings.

Down the road would be a paper with her as one of the co-authors.

"This is exciting, both of us getting to work for Dr. Royal. I'm sure she wants to help you in the class, too, and this is part of a larger plan for you."

"Oh, I hope so!" Diana pulled her legs up now also, hugging her knees and closing her eyes dreamily. "She really is so, sooo nice."

Mid thought of her brother who closed his eyes in missionary fantasies. He would tell Mid he saw himself bringing Christianity to people in tropical countries no white man had visited. He would be loved and return to receive his father's praise-- perhaps even an apology for doubting his sincerity.

Mid also remembered the look on Bill's face when he talked about nearly drowning in Greenwood Lake. For half a minute he had left this world on his way to the next, traveling in spirit to wherever God was.

"So," Mid asked, "when do I report to our scientific leader?'

"First thing Monday, as soon as your classes are over, of course."

Up until this moment Mid hadn't thought about when Professor Royal had talked to Diana about this project.

"And you talked to her . . . Friday?"

"Oh, no. Today. She came to see me. Right here in Close Hall. Can you believe it? Everyone was so surprised . . . to find out . . . well, that I'm important."

She looked up. "*We're* important, I mean! We'll be a team, the subjects of a physiology program."

Mid waited a moment, then asked, "I thought you said she called you into her office?"

"Well, she took me to her office. After she came here. We went together, talking about our childhoods. Did you know her grandmother was a nurse in the Civil War?"

"I didn't. But that might account for her going into physiology, a tradition in the family."

The story of Corporal Miles replayed in Mid's mind, the wounded soldier who believed he'd been a musician. Was poor Diana another project of Dr. Royal, who would guide her away from insecurity to a satisfaction with her limitations? Mid believed her own patience with her lab partner was working to the same end.

"Her Grandmother lived with her and taught her all sorts of things. My Grandma still lives on her own farm, raises chickens and sells the eggs, riding into town on her mule." Diana grimaced. "She's an ornery one, I told Professor Royal. And Professor Royal said I'd never have to live on my own and work that way. I have a future!"

Why, wondered Mid, did the teacher share her childhood stories with Diana and not with her? Grandmother Woodruff had come from Germany and started life all over again in a new country. She was a model for the three Lacy sisters. Well, Mid was convinced, when she met Dr. Royal on Monday, they'd share such stories.

It turned out, however, that Mid learned they might share a future more than a past. She was being recruited in a research project that would set a course neither she nor any member of her family had anticipated.

Chapter Seventeen: Back Home

Although she didn't recognize the little moments of emptiness for what they were that fall, Marian missed her parents.

Perhaps because, throughout her childhood, her father was gone to work so early in the morning and was not back until well into the evening, she believed she was accustomed to his absence. And her mother's retreat into books and letters made her seem less present in the house than the grandparents. She assumed she would miss Alice, and Bill, of course, who were constantly with her. But she had unconsciously concluded not seeing Mother and Father daily at Archer would be just a repeat of what it had been like on Ridge Road.

As the academic term moved into winter months, however--the days becoming shorter and darker-- Mid found herself imagining scenes from home as if they were nearby and she would soon appear in the midst of her family. Her relationship to Glenna, initially intense, had slipped into a static state. Her roommate was often on the prowl, while Mid stayed in to study. They continued to play bridge, though not always as partners.

Of course, the small size of Archer and the nature of the institution as a women's school meant you were never really alone. Everyone ate in the dining hall at the same times; most attended weekly chapel despite varying degrees of interest; and the library was a focal point for chatter as much as study in between classes and in the evenings.

Loneliness, then, was not what Marian felt. And she had no desire to retreat from college back to Rutherford. Still, some deep underpinning had slipped away from her somehow, and she couldn't put her finger on what she needed to feel grounded.

When Tony called to ask when he could come to campus, his talk of family may have triggered a suspicion that being away from home was the cause of her malaise.

"You've been to see your parents, then?" she asked when he explained he'd been back in this country nearly a month. As she spoke she saw in her mind's eye their adjoining back yards, the Giordano's second floor visible from the Lacy girls' room, two parallel walkways from porch to street out front. She could often guess at activities inside the house next door, especially in the summers when windows were open and stray sounds wandered across the fence.

"No, not yet. We've written. And I called when I first got off the ship, just so they'd be sure I was really in America."

Mid hesitated, but then felt it necessary to ask, "Were you . . . where there is fighting going on . . . were you hurt? Is that why you're here in Maryland, for treatment?"

"That's part of it, yes." His voice was strained, and she felt it might have been better not to have brought up the topic. "I'll explain everything when I come to Archer. I'm all right, though. I want you to know that." He gave an unhappy little laugh. "There are no gaping wounds, I have all my limbs."

"Well, that's good. You looked . . . maybe, a bit thin, but I could tell it was you, at the Hippodrome. I was . . . just not expecting you. Anyway, if you present yourself at the porter's office, by the main gate, they'll direct you to Close Hall. There you speak to Mrs. Wrenn, the housekeeper. I'll come down to get you."

Mid decided to take Tony to The Gather as a public location, distinct from the realm of her private Archer existence. Recalling his haggard look at the Hippodrome, she was uncertain about how he might behave. If Dr. Royal's patient Corporal Miles, who'd fantasized a musician's past, had been shellshocked, perhaps Tony was suffering from something similar. She would also take her knitting bag with her, as a distraction, should she need one.

He didn't seem to be distressed, however, when she met him in the lobby. He was reserved but clearly pleased to see her. And for the first hour in The Gather he kept the conversation on Rutherford matters relayed in his mother's recent letters. It seemed Mrs. Giordano knew more about the Lacy family than she did!

"Bill wants to travel up the Yangtse with nothing but a Bible and good intentions."

"Father will never let him go."

"Not with China fighting Japan! My brother says he pays no attention to what's in the papers. His mental map of the world is marked only by territories unclaimed by the church."

Mid's internal geography contained vast swaths of space she would never visit.

"I looked at a map of Spain a few weeks ago. We were studying the Moors in our civilization course. And then the Inquisition. There's a lot of history where . . . where you were."

He looked at the wall of bookshelves on one wall of The Gather. "Yes, but I didn't learn much about the past while I was there. When you're with an army, even a ragtag group of workers, what you see are vantage points, escape routes, shelter from fire."

Mid looked at him carefully. Was he getting to the subject he really wanted to talk about? What it was like to be in an uprising. Or was he going to say he was through with his overseas adventures and renew his proposal of marriage to her?

She asked, "I hope you're home to stay now?"

He was deliberate in his response. "No, no, I don't think so. I didn't experience what I went for."

"Oh?"

"It was . . . strange," he said. Again his gaze wandered away from her, over the books, at the windows. "The real fighting was always off in the distance, you know, the other side of the city, down by the river, in the next town. Sometimes I would hear the gunfire . . . or echoes of it. It was hard to tell what was happening and where it was."

Mid thought of the country around Greenwood Lake, where thunderstorms could be farther up in the mountains but the rumbling would travel down valleys so you weren't sure if it was close or far. And if the water was still, especially at dusk or dawn, whispers would slide along the surface. Were the speakers on the other shore or on your side but half a mile away?

"A small group of us were being held in reserve," Tony went on, his eyes focused now on that scene, not in The Gather. "We didn't think we'd be called on, something about the larger uprising and that this was only supposed to be a skirmish anyway."

He paused again, looking down at his hands. They lay limply on his thighs, as if they too didn't know whether they'd be called to immediate action or left there for some future event. Mid couldn't tell if she should prompt him to go on or try to change the subject.

"There was an explosion, I'm pretty sure. I saw a flash and heard a . . . a bang. But, really, the next thing I knew I was lying in an ambulance. They were lifting me on my stretcher to take me to hospital."

"You mean you'd been shot? You were bleeding?"

"No . . . no. I had a . . . concussion. The blast-- dynamite, a grenade, I don't know--came from behind me, threw me into the wall of a little shed, apparently. That's what they told me later. For a long time at hospital I . . . I couldn't remember much of anything. I knew my name, but not why I was where I was, what I had been doing."

Again, Mid was at a loss about what to say, or what not to say.

"So," he said, sitting up straight, patting his thighs with his hands, focusing his gaze, a smile of sorts on his face. "So, I went off to fight and didn't feel anything. Didn't see the enemy, didn't fire a gun, didn't . . . didn't take any action except to fly headlong into a building."

"Well, now, that's not doing nothing," she protested. "You volunteered, you went there. Not everyone plays the role . . . " She was going to say the role of the hero. " . . . the role of the man on the front lines, the one who sees the whites of their eyes."

"Yes, they told me that. At the hospital, once I began to come around, to remember . . . well, eventually I remembered everything except the moment I was . . . injured. And, of course, at Fort Meade, it's been reassuring."

"I bet your family wants you to stay here. You were such a good student, and went to that summer institute. You should be in college."

He scanned the room again. "It's nice here. You like it?"

"Oh, yes. I mean, I'm still getting used to things, the different girls, from all over, really. And I'm not sure what I'll study after the first two years. But there's so much to learn. And the professors . . . well, they know ever so much." She thought of Dr. Royal and the odd meeting she'd had with her the day before.

Tony looked closely at her. "Mom says your mother has gotten a telegram, something official, it might be from the government. She called me last night and said perhaps you should know. Mrs. Lacy, your mother, seemed pretty upset about whatever the telegram said."

Chapter Eighteen: Lines

Telephoning home was out of the question: the Lacys were too frugal. She might have sent a telegram asking her parents about what Tony had said, but that, too, would be considered excessive. Mid knew, if they thought she needed to be informed, they'd find the appropriate way. So she waited for a letter, if not from her parents, at least from Alice. She would concentrate on her new role as research assistant for Dr. Royal's study of the female form.

Rather than encourage Tony to visit her at Archer again, she urged him to return to Rutherford, where, she insisted again, his family would need him. He said he had only a few more sessions at the hospital (he did not say what "sessions" meant or what kind of hospital this was) and would probably be on a train early the following week. But he was determined, after a suitable period of rest, to return to war.

When she met with Dr. Royal in her office, Mid had been surprised to see the Dean of Students there as well. She would learn over the coming weeks that Jaqueline Dupont had been one of the Hello Girls of World War I, and she had a special interest in Dr. Royal's work.

In late 1917, when General Pershing made a call for bilingual telephone operators to improve communication in the trenches, Jacqueline responded. She had grown up in a large family of

French immigrants south of St. Louis, and, although her parents spoke English well, they insisted their children use the native language at home. Jacqueline had wanted to see more of the world, even if it involved travel to war-torn Europe.

While the military saw Hello Girls as go-betweens--linking British-American-French troops on front lines with French-American-British commanders in the rear--Jacqueline had asserted herself in a different capacity: she connected the civilian populations of two countries and, in that small act, contributed to the international understanding of the Great War's human cost. Writing home from the front, she told family and friends what she experienced.

While other Hello Girls often lost their composure when messages were being sent and received during battle, she had demonstrated such calm that she was moved steadily closer to the action. There were even several occasions when she was so close to the shelling that, with no one available to go forward and repair severed telephone wires, she snatched up a tool kit and did the job herself.

What she witnessed in her work contradicted the propaganda she'd read in her training and in newspaper accounts she'd seen before enlisting. Her dispassionate letters showing the randomness of death and the soldiers' bewilderment about their mission added to the growing civilian awareness of the tragedy of the conflict, the literal slaughter of a generation.

As time went on she got to know several French families living in villages near where she was quartered. They, of course, already understood what she was learning. To give them a small outlet for their sorrow and helplessness, she matched individuals in France and Missouri as pen pals. Writing and reading seemed to offer a small measure of relief and gave Jacqueline a sense that she had helped humanity end a kind of mass suicide.

Returning home after the war, Jacqueline was frustrated that jobs she could have handled went to men and ones she was offered paid far less than she'd earned in France. (The salaries for Hello Girls had been equivalent to what male soldiers doing similar tasks were paid.) So, after a year, she left home for Fort Meade a second time, where she enlisted the aid of an officer she'd served with. Using contacts he had established over a long career, he negotiated a position for her as administrative aide to the Physiology Department at Archer. By the time Mid arrived some years later, she was managing the labs for all sciences and was often called on by the college president to handle sensitive special projects.

Mid had seen Ms. Dupont around the campus but always as a part of the background--another figure on stage at chapel, the person Mrs. Wrenn met with on a weekly basis, the woman who checked the dining hall menu for balanced food groups. Now, it seemed, she was consulting with Dr. Royal.

"Do you know Dean Dupont?" Dr. Royal asked, Turning to the Dean, however, she didn't leave time for Mid to respond. "Miss Lacy is a capable student in my introductory course, and I believe she can keep the records of our girls."

Mid would like to have been more than "capable." Still, perhaps it was better to be keeping records than to be just one of the "girls."

She looked more closely at the Dean, who, though a small, slight person, stood straight and looked directly at her with an intensity that almost made her uncomfortable.

"You're from New Jersey, aren't you," Ms. Dupont said. "Why have you come all this way to school? Please sit."

Mid took the chair she gestured toward. "My father thought it would be good for me . . . academically."

"And your father . . . ?"

"He's the chief financial officer in a marine insurance company, in New York."

"That industry is in for difficult times, but aren't we all!" She cleared her throat in what seemed a prelude to a new topic, but did not move from her stationary pose. "Miss Lacy, we have an important project we'd like you to be involved in, one that could bring Archer some recognition, as well as funds which are vital for our college's future."

"I'm quite eager to help. I so like Dr. Royal's class. I want to study physiology." She hadn't thought so until this moment, but the idea of working with these impressive women was beginning to go to her head.

"What Dr. Royal is doing, with President Gloucester's support, is proving that women have more stamina than has been generally recognized. They have the capacity to endure physical strain, and they have powers of concentration that have not been utilized in our industrial society. But their abilities are vital to the fate of this country."

Mid's eyes widened. She wondered if she was going to be asked to swim across the Bay or hike up Quirauk Mountain. And what threat had she failed to see all around her?

Dr. Royal took up the story. "Scientific descriptions of women's physical capabilities are flawed, the result of measurements made by men in contexts that failed to challenge us. What you read in textbooks--even the one we're using in class--still derives from data collected in the last century from studies of undernourished factory girls, women pampered by servants, and mothers weakened by multiple child births. Well, many of their subjects were also weakened by . . . by men who . . . who drink."

Mid could not take in what her professor was saying. Women were not as everyone assumed? Her mother could have carried supplies to Camp Robin on her back if needed? Grandmother's rules about resting in the afternoon and not roughhousing with boys were based on false premises?

"No one has used as test subjects healthy farm girls, the New Woman who rides a bicycle and plays tennis, women who accompany missionaries to remote places where they have to use their physical strengths to survive."

"We're building a new model of women's physiology that will be critical for the time ahead. You know, I assume, that this country is headed toward war. And we'll need every able-bodied citizen to work as hard as possible to protect our way of life."

Mid thought nobody in this country wanted to go war. Let Europe battle for their empires; we should take care of ourselves. She had dismissed Tony's military adventure as a boyish impulse, little better than a prank to get attention. She knew her father was opposed to war.

"Your friend, Miss Tracy--Diana Tracy--is one of three girls we have identified at Archer with unusual physical qualities. Ruth Montgomery, a senior history major, and Mary Hobarts, a junior student of home economics, are the other two specimens. We are going to put them through a battery of tests and record their performances--both in the field, where we'll measure such things as speed, agility, strength--and in the laboratory, where we'll calibrate their oxygen use, their metabolism, their heart rate--all standard indicators of underlying physical ability."

"I'll be honored to do what I can," Mid said in a subdued voice. It sounded, though, as if she were going to be a glorified secretary, recording the achievements of others.

"You'll be doing more than note-taking for this project, Miss Lacy. You will be coaching these three girls to excel at what they do. And you face a serious

130

obstacle: they don't get along. However, we feel you have the skills to bring out the best in each without turning them against one another. If you're successful--and we depend on you to be successful--in the end, young lady, you are going to help create a warrior race of women, Amazons for the modern age."

Chapter 19: Goods

So Marian was once again the one in the middle, neither at the heart of the matter nor so far away that she was free to ignore what was happening. Not researcher or subject, she was to lose herself in joining types. She would pull together a potentially contentious group of girls, each of whom possessed a talent needed by the world. But if she succeeded, what became of her and her conciliatory powers? A kind of catalyst, Mid would be consumed in the creation of the "Fit Female," as Dr. Royal occasionally referred to her objective.

In an odd, indirect way, however, Mid would later feel her true destiny had been visible in the sequence of events that fall, highlighted by connections with Fort Meade. Dean Dupont, who had trained at that navy base, and Tony Giodano, who had been treated there, linked her to a military installation whose former name would be a fixture in her adult life.

In 1928 Camp Meade had been designated "Fort Leonard Wood" after the only doctor to have been the Army's Chief of Staff. A congressman from Pennsylvania, however, blocked appropriations for the base under that name because George Meade was a native son of his state, and he perceived the decision to rename the base a slight. So, in 1929 it became Fort Meade again.

However, Leonard Wood, whose distinguished service included winning the Medal of Honor, was later recognized in the naming of a major training facility in south central Missouri. In 1949 Mid would move to Fairfield, thirty minutes east on famous Route 66 from Fort Leonard Wood, to begin raising her family. Near Fort Meade in one time of peace and close to Fort Leonard Wood in another, she moved through years of war to discover who she really was.

At Archer she continued to hope her future was overseas. She felt the Fit Female project might, in fact, help her in that direction. Glenna, for one, was impressed, especially when Mid reported some of the official language of the experiment; "'In order to dismantle the frame of feeble femininity to which women have all been consigned--by men, of course-- we will employ strict discipline, a precise reward system, and the latest in scientific equipment.'"

"My father would scoff at such an idea. Therefore, I love it! How are you quantifying your results?"

Glenna was lounging in the chair at her desk, feet propped on one corner. She claimed she had to study for a British literature exam, but, as usual, it was easy to distract her with almost any topic.

Mid explained, "We have all sorts of instruments-- respirometers, kymographs, sphygmomanometers. And there are charts, graphs, data tables. They've been getting ready for this for quite a while, but now they feel there's a urgency . . . because of the war they're certain is coming."

"They're all worked up about nothing, just like Tim."

"You've been talking to Tim . . . Jensen? Did he call for me?"

Mid recalled how he--like Tony, the Dean, and Dr. Royal--was concerned with what was happening in Europe. Maybe there *were* reasons to see a future for herself outside the United States.

Glenna looked toward the window. "No, I . . . I saw him at another of the Hopkins parties. We got into a longwinded discussion of nurses and doctors, why the doctors are all men, the nurses women."

"I was supposed to read a book he lent me." Mid scanned her shelf, but didn't see *Das Kapital*.

"Oh, I borrowed it. You hadn't been exactly captivated by it, so . . . after I finished it, I gave it back to him."

"You saw him again, after the party?"

Glenna dropped her feet from the desktop, scanned the bookshelves herself as if *Das Kapital* might still be there somewhere.

"We've had coffee in Federal Hill a few times. I met some friends of his--interesting people. Although he's the one who . . . who interests me."

Glenna shifted from her desk chair to her bed, throwing her head back on the pillow and crossing her feet at the other end. "You know, my mother was a nurse. She retired when I was born. And my father has gone through dozens of nurses in his practice. He's pretty hard on them, so not many stay very long."

"Tim would tell them to organize, wouldn't he. Rise up against the oppressor."

Glenna laughed. "Of course. And I might say the same thing, if I ever thought I'd be in the medical profession."

Mid recalled her discussion with Tim about Negroes at the Hopkins party, his assumption that she understood those who held inferior positions.

Glenna sat up and looked at her roommate. "By the way, Tim's going to be calling for you this Saturday night."

"He is? Oh, dear! I should have read his book! Did he explain why he was coming?

"Actually, Mild, he's coming to see me, but he'll call for you."

"For me? Why?"

Glenna gave her hoarse chuckle. "He believes I have something that possesses 'surplus value.' And the only way . . . the only for him to obtain it is to pretend he's your guest at Archer."

Mid puzzled at this. "What does 'surplus value' mean?"

"Well, as I understand it, it involves something whose price is far above the cost of the labor needed to produce it and deliver it to a customer, with appropriate profit to those involved."

"It's price is too far from its value?"

"That's right. The commodity is desired beyond its worth--'surplus value'--because of flawed social systems, not inherent quality. And the unscrupulous few who understand this process exploit the ignorant many who desire products they don't need."

"But, you're not going to sell your . . . whatever it is that has surplus value?"

"Honey, my high priced goods have already been sold, but Tim doesn't know that."

Mid shook her head. "I'm completely confused."

Glenna reached toward her roommate. "Mild, may you stay so for a long, long time!"

Again, Mid wondered at the odd statements of her unconventional friend. She thought about another of the ideas Dr. Royal had pointed out to her. Women are not only thought to be weaker physically than they are, she'd explained, but also mentally. Conventional wisdom says they can't reason in complex ways. That's why there are so few female mathematicians, inventors, politicians. Their brains are smaller than men's, and this dictates that their appropriate sphere of responsibility be the domestic. Their emotional capacity and moral sense can function in the home, but not outside it. Glenna didn't seem to fit that mold.

Mid returned to the fact that Tim would call for her, but want something from Glenna.

"Okay, so when Tim calls, what do I do?"

"You take him to The Gather for awhile. He'll probably be carrying another book for you to read and explain how important it is. Then, at some point, he'll suggest the two of you take a walk around the campus, see the sites."

"You know there's not much you don't go past just by coming to Close Hall."

"I understand. So . . . so, what you do is walk a bit, then excuse yourself . . . um, near the library. Say you have to powder your nose."

"My nose?"

"Yes. But take some time to do it. Oh, about half an hour. You can stay in there or go read a magazine. It doesn't matter. But, when you come out, he'll be waiting for you."

"Wait a minute. While I'm in the library, is he going to do something he shouldn't, something that will get me in trouble."

"I'll be the one who gets in trouble if anyone does!"

"But, while I'm in the library, he'll be meeting you?"

"Yes, that's it. We're meeting to talk about the roles of doctors and nurses, employers and workers, producers and consumers."

This was making less and less sense. Why couldn't Glenna receive him at Close, then take him to The Gather, if their goal was political discussion?

"Where is this meeting going to take place?"

"Well, it'll be in Baltimore, to be sure." Glenna smiled and pivoted on the bed to look out the window. Then she added a fuller explanation, a phrase at a time, each bracketed by provocative pauses: "On the Archer campus. In Close Hall. In this room. On my bed."

Chapter 20: Family Ties

Marian would tell her children years later that she never made an A in her college career. She made few C's, but could never reach the top in one of her courses.

"The one time I stayed up all night to study for a final exam, I scored the lowest I ever had on a test."

"You pulled an 'all-nighter'?" questioned Curtis. He was in college then himself, and the practice was routine in his set. "That doesn't sound like you."

Mid smiled. "No, I'm pretty regular in my habits, partly because that's the way your father likes it, but also because raising two boys required organization."

Karl had fit comfortably into a fixed family routine, so Curtis knew she was referring to him as the agent of disorder.

"What was the class?"

"Advanced Human Anatomy. I was so close to making an A, a 94.5 point average. The professor told me, if I turned in a strong performance on my lab journal and at the final, I would have an A. So, I drank ten cups of coffee, took walks outside in the cold air to wake up, never let myself get horizontal until the sun came up."

Glenna had helped, though they were no longer roommates in their senior year. She had made so many A's, she was sure she could coach Mild to this one.

"So, which part did you mess up on, the lab or the exam?"

"Both. I fell asleep an hour before the time and had to take a cold shower to shock my system into life. Still, I was ten minutes late. And the lab report had simple errors I was too tired to catch."

"You . . . you didn't fail the course, did you?"

"Oh, no. I got my usual B. I'd built up a cushion, so I couldn't fall too low. That was usually true in my school work. No low grades, no high grades, just respectable, middle level of achievement."

Karl and their father had both been excellent students, seldom failing to make A's. Curtis generally did very well or very poorly. It all depended on whether he liked the course, or the professor. He would strive all his life to achieve consistency, but never quite get there.

Mid understood the erratic performance of her younger son, perhaps because of the contrast with her own behavior . . . or at least with the pattern her immediate family knew. In the 1950s, regularity was highly valued, especially in the community surrounding an engineering college. She took advantage of scientific advances--household appliances like her washing machine and vacuum cleaner, processed foods (Wonder Bread and Carnation Milk), national prosperity (cheap gas and electricity)--to keep her household in a reassuring routine.

There had been, however, some years after college when she fluctuated between brief periods of steady employment, longer times of unfulfilling volunteer work, and intense bouts of depression from which she retreated, first to Greenwood Lake, then, with her mother to a cottage near West Milford. Some of her anguish during those years came from imagining travel to distant places. But some came from the long wartime journey she actually did endure.

At Archer she began to accept the barriers that stood between her and that wider world. First, there were the conventions that constrained women's movements. Then came her father's strictness. (After Ella eloped, he was even more determined to keep Mid and Alice by his side until they married men he approved.) Finally, Mid lamented, there seemed to be something about herself, about who she was, that led to her being passed over when opportunities arose. Someone older or younger, taller or shorter, smarter or less able would be selected instead of her, even though she possessed whatever skill or talent was required.

She would think often about Dr. Paterson's poetic image of her as a child, created when he believed she would not survive into adulthood. In his imagination she had been transformed from sick girl to angel rising to heaven, her life as a grownup bypassed by a fatal disease.

In reality she had come back from illness to this world and a regular existence. The piece of paper her mother had tucked back into a family photo album, however, convinced Marian that she had a special destiny, that she had been called from the realm of the spirit to play a role in this world's affairs. She had gone to Archer convinced that the foundations of her new identity awaited her there.

The day after Glenna's rendezvous with Tim Jensen, Mid sat on her bed, looking at her father's steamer trunk, the metal box in which she'd packed everything needed for her college career. The stickers seemed now to identify places she would never go----Buenos Aires, Venice, Bangkok. She would watch Fit Females depart to other laboratories or to special training centers, while she remained in Baltimore, completing records and filing forms.

She looked at her roommate's empty bed, now neatly made. Glenna told her at lunch that she would be in for bed check after dinner, but not to look for her again until early the next morning. She had done more in this room (surplus value) and outside it (through her window escape) than Mid expected to experience until she was married . . . if she married.

So, what was she to do for three and half more years? Live vicariously through the adventures of her fellow students? Or plan for a change?

Well, her father was taking her to St. Louis in another month. They would be gone for ten days, crossing the country by train and seeing a city bordered on three sides by water. Would she be an American Lo-tsen, descending from the ancient peace of a mountain monastery into the hectic clashes of modernity? Only if she escaped her father's control, perhaps on a river boat. The great Missouri joined the Mississippi on the city's north, and the strong Meramec came in to the merging waters just south of the metropolitan area.

She heard a knock and looked up to see Diana peering shyly around her door. "There's a . . . a telegram for you." She held up an envelope, the words "Western Union" visible. "I hope it's okay, but I signed for you . . . because, well, because we're together, on a team."

"Oh, sure. Yes," Mid said, though she was startled at what felt like an invasion of privacy. While the envelope was sealed, her lab partner had crossed a line to an intimacy with which Mid was not yet comfortable.

Diana came into the room to hand her the telegram, then plumped down on the steamer trunk. "I hope it's not bad news. It could just be money from your folks, couldn't it? For the holiday trip home. I have to take the bus. Well, as far as Hagarstown. Then stay with my uncle until another bus goes on to Elkins. There my father can come get me, though it takes five hours each way."

Mid opened the telegram, which was succinct: "Your uncle found in Lyndhurst. All well. Mother." She read it twice, searching for additional meaning.

"What? Oh, do tell," begged Diana. "Is everyone all right? Is it just the money order?"

Mid folded up the telegram and forced herself to smile. "It's . . . ah, my uncle . . . we hadn't heard from him for . . . for some time. And we were worried. But he's fine. He . . . he had been ill on a business trip. But, he's back home now, and Mother wanted me to know."

142

Diana's face brightened. "Well, that's good news, then. Everybody is all right. They just didn't want you to be upset, of course. Or to be surprised when you came home. That's nice, so nice that they've sent . . . a telegram."

Her mother's words had been, as always, carefully chosen. A writer herself, a skillful player at word games like charades, she had given her daughter a simple statement but one with complex meaning. Ethel's brother Henry "found" in Lyndhurst: he'd been there, then, a long time, perhaps ever since his disappearance. Lyndhurst was just south of Rutherford, hardly in the area of Montreal where the train he had supposedly been on was derailed. Rather than far away from his family all those years, then, he was right next door?

"All well": that would mean Henry was well, of course, but who was included in "all": Mid's parents and siblings, probably; but did Henry, a bachelor when he left on a business trip, now have his own family, a different "all"? And did "well" mean simply healthy, comfortable, secure? Or did this refer to state of mind. Would Henry's presence now within the Woodruff family cause emotional distress or perhaps disturb existing relationships and priorities? How would Nana, whose silence about her son had always been puzzling, react to this news?

One thing was certain: she would not know what this telegram meant until she got off the train in Rutherford two weeks from tomorrow. Until then she would be occupying herself with introductory physiology, the duties of a Fit Female coach, and the gnawing fear that a life of meaning might be harder to achieve than she'd imagined.

Set above the main entrance to the Headhouse of Union Station at the time Mid traveled with her father to St. Louis was a striking, allegorical window. She'd read about it in a guide book Glenna loaned her. Leaving the station, she turned back to scan the composition, a key element in the design of architect, Theodore Link.

Her father also looked up at the hand-cut, stained glass figures and smiled. "There are my girls." Mid was shocked: a thousand miles from home, she was still defined by others?

She had learned that the three forms represented train stations in New York, St. Louis, and San Francisco, busiest in the nation. But Father transformed them into Mid flanked by two other women, Alice and Ella. The sisters on the left and right were the ends of a continuum, with Mid just a reference point to their distinctive identities.

To give the women in the window more control of their identities, she posed an alternative interpretation: "They might be the three Fates, Father, weaving past, present, and future."

"Perhaps." Father turned around and gestured for a taxi. "But they're so beautiful, I prefer to see them as lovely young women that men adore--Ella, Marian, and Alice." Mid sighed, praying she would not be stuck in anyone else's picture so far from home.

On the Wednesday of that week, however, she read about another woman trapped in a man's picture and feared she was a similar victim. In a quaint bookstore near Memorial Plaza, she was shopping for picture post cards to mail home when saw a collection of writings by Mark Twain, Missouri's most famous literary son. She was struck by an essay he wrote for the December 1912 *Harper's Magazine*, which was displayed on a store rack.

She had read *Tom Sawyer* in school. And her literary-minded mother recommended other Twain books, aware that, at one point, the Brooklyn library had banned *Huckleberry Finn*. But Twain's little known "My Platonic Sweetheart" haunted her for years.

"Do you believe in dreams?" asked an attractive young man who was also looking at the Twain display.

"Pardon?" By instinct, she clutched her purse more tightly under her arm.

"That story you're looking at, the one by Twain. It's about a recurring dream he had. And the way you were looking at it, I wondered if you've had visions of . . . of the people who . . . who will be in your future."

The boy had a dreamy look himself. She decided he was not someone to fear.

"Oh, I don't know exactly," she responded, smiling at his enthusiasm. "I tend to think our dreams are made up of the past, images inspired by what we've already seen or done."

146

He took the magazine gently from her, turned a few pages, and read: "'*In our dreams — I know it! — we do make the journeys we seem to make; we do see the things we seem to see; . . . they are living spirits, not shadows; and they are immortal and indestructible.*'"

She shrugged. "This could just be one of Twain's exaggerated tales, a fantasy."

"Do you know what the main figure of his dream was?"

"No." Then looking at the title, she offered: "His sweetheart?"

"Exactly! But not a real girl from his childhood, or his wife, or anyone he'd met. She was someone he . . . he encountered, many times over the course of his life. A kind of ideal. Platonic. A dream person, like an angel."

Mid frowned, recalling herself in Dr. Paterson's poem, a child who had died and was rising toward heaven in the words of her mother's friend. She decided to switch the topic to the boy. "Do you have a dream sweetheart, too?"

He blushed. "I don't know. I have thought about the . . . the girl I'd like to meet one day, what she would look like, how she would walk, the sound of her voice."

Cocking her head coyly, Mid said, "But, so far . . . ?" Then she moved head a little to the left, a little to the right, as if trying to catch his eye.
"I . . . I haven't seen her, though there are some girls that . . . that might be close."

He was looking directly at her now, smiling.

"In 1912," (she read the date on the magazine), "Mark Twain would have been an old man, wouldn't he? If he was going to meet his dream girl, he'd have done so by then. Really, he should have met her when he was . . . oh, about your age."

He hesitated. "In his dreams, Twain was always seventeen, and the girl was fifteen. He claimed he met her about once every two years, but they were always the same ages. She adored him, of course. They were like brother and sister, but even more . . . even closer somehow."

Mid was conscious of how close she was to this boy, who had moved over to hold the magazine and show her passages. Stepping back, she asked, "Do you go to school here?"

"No, I'm just visiting. I live in Kansas, but my grandparents are in Jefferson City. We're visiting. I used money I earned last summer to come to St. Louis for a day."

"To see the sights?"

"To get a taste of . . . the big city. They had the World's Fair here back in 1904. You can tour the buildings in Forest Park. Have you been?"

"No, I live in New Jersey, just across the river from New York, in Rutherford. I'm here for a few days with my father. He's on a business trip."

His eyes widened. "New York! The biggest city in the world! It must be exciting."

"It is, but . . . but there's not really that much opportunity there, for me."

148

He didn't notice her reservation. "They're planning a new park here, the Jefferson National Expansion Memorial. It will celebrate the joining of East and West, the Louisiana Purchase."

"This is my first time west of the Mississippi. I'm . . . I'm expanding my own horizons."

His eyes glowed. "Oh, me, too. I'm going to do great things. I'll be a scientist like Albert Einstein. He proved that time and space are not finite."

"Um?"

"Someday we'll travel through time. We'll have no limits to where we can be."

Limits, thought Marian, sadly. That's what's real for me, boundaries I can't cross. Great things are to the left of me, to the right, behind, in front, but not where I am. They're always over there, back here, around somewhere. I exist as a dream girl held in suspension by men. They are free to take me where they will, but I don't travel on my own.

"Come with me," the boy said impetuously. "Let's go to the site of the World's Fair. The slogan was 'Open ye gates. Swing wide, ye portals.' Let's pass through, right now."

For a moment, Mid was strangely tempted. The boy's eyes were bright, his eagerness appealing. And he was just an innocent, star struck boy. What would be the harm?

But then her inner voice--the balanced, temperate, composed self that was always in control--told Mid she couldn't. Her father expected her in less than an hour. This boy was a complete stranger. She didn't know if there even was such a place as a World's Fair.

Impetuously, though, she took his hand. "Thank you, thank you for asking me; that's so kind. But . . . but I can't. I don't . . . I don't do things . . . on impulse. Still, . . . thank you." She took the magazine from his hand and returned it to the rack, smiled, and walked out of the store.

"In 1930," Father explained two days later, "the census showed that the geographic midpoint of the nation was just north of Linton." He was gesturing out the window in the dining car, a map of Indiana spread out on the table between them. She had been writing in her journal.

"The middle of the country?" She knew that St. Louis was only a third of the distance across the continent, so, they couldn't be halfway between East and West Coasts.

"No, the center of the people--the men, women, and children of the United States."

"Ah."

Father continued. "Of course, the midpoint is moving--west and south, as people look for new places of opportunity, more space to live. By 1940, they say it will be closer to Carlisle." He turned the map around so she could see." They were approaching Terra Haute, perhaps twenty miles north of the two little towns.

Mid had read about farmers fleeing the Dust Bowl for states where rainfall was predictable and the soil better for crops, swelling their populations.

Jobs were not plentiful in eastern manufacturing cities, as bank failures and stock losses were still forcing businesses to cut back. Even the prospect of a European war--and potentially higher demand for American products--was not ending the Depression. Exodus south and west.

Had she passed the midpoint of her life on this trip? Was the moment of choice, the pivotal chance, sliding west and south away from her? Would she look back at the day a boy asked her to break away as the one instance in her life that opportunity appeared and she passed it by?

Volume Three: As the Crow Flies.
Chapter 21: Blood

The late afternoon sun breaking through clouds above St. Anne's Hospital in Passaic illuminated a single drop of liquid suspended from the pipette. "Life or death?" Marian wondered, knowing that the test she was about to perform could say one or the other. She took a personal interest in the results, as she not only knew the man whose blood she was examining: she loved him.

Releasing the second drop onto the slide, Marian thought of Dr. Paterson's lab, a basement room in his own office on Ridge Road. There, some years ago, a drop of her own blood had meant death for a young girl, daughter of the doctor's friend--or so he had believed. Had the test been accurate, she would not be alive today, holding her breath with anxiety.

Marian, as a summer laboratory technologist's assistant, wanted to think of herself as one of the three sisters of Fate, determining the future of patients. Since she still carried knitting with her wherever she went, the role of weaver of destinies seemed appropriate. Today, with such personal interest in the results, she prayed that her hand would spin out a long life for her uncle.

In the two and half years since his "discovery" in Lyndhurst, Henry and Marian had become close. Father had been suspicious of his brother-in-law's story at first. But Mid, looking into her uncle's eyes as he narrated what had happened, knew it to be true. And, after all he had endured, she could not believe his life would be cut short.

When Mother learned that her brother had survived and was in Lyndhurst, she immediately remembered the prediction of Frances Border and what happened in 1917 to the Canadian Car and Foundry Company in a neighboring town. Half a million shells had exploded, destroying an entire plant. Ethel's memory of that event had framed a vision of her brother's tragic fate. She explained what it was like to her family at dinner one night during the Christmas vacation.

"We could hear the noise, the booming. It was as if the war in Europe had crossed the Atlantic and was in our backyard."

"What caused it?" Mid asked.

"I don't think they ever found out, but, in a munitions plant, one mishap and everything can go." Ever since Henry's disappearance, she had connected him with such a horrific scene--train crash or fiery collapse. Alice asked if people were killed.

"That's the amazing part: no deaths. There was a woman switchboard operator--I don't remember her name--but she saved everyone, over a thousand people."

"She directed them to safety?" asked Bill.

"Yes, she called the fire departments, the police, and then each of the buildings, one by one. She didn't leave her post until she had contacted them all. 'Get out or go up!' she told them. They believed her and escaped. She was a hero."

Ethel didn't know that one of the shells actually came into the operators' office. Still, she continued to contact every building. When she was done, she could barely walk from the strain of the emergency and had to be helped to safety herself.

Mid recalled the Hello Girls and Dean Dupont, who had also stayed at her post as a telephone operator in a time of danger. She had been in the trenches of World War I. Now she was a key figure at Archer College and in a larger movement to change the roles of women. Mid wanted to be like her, doing more than pass on messages, even if they were critical. She almost wanted to rush into a building and drag people out of danger. At the very least, she wanted to be someplace where fires might break out, where leaders could emerge.

"I'm going into the medical field," she announced. "I don't want to be a teacher any more."

"Oh?" Father raised his eyebrows, suggesting that he would be the one to decide.

"Yes, I . . . I have begun to work in a laboratory at school, in a research program. I can major in physiology and go on to become a medical technologist."

Mid hadn't told Dr. Royal of this decision yet. In fact, it was taking shape over this break from school, in part because of her uncle's story.

Twenty years earlier, a review at Starr's Railroad Shipping Company revealed that several thousands dollars were missing. Three people were implicated: Christopher Cunningham, the bookkeeper; an account manager, Henry Woodruff; and his boss, Raymond Starr, the owner's son. Henry believed the other two had worked together to implicate him, the man in the middle. But he had no way to prove his innocence. To avoid an arrest he believed was inevitable, he bought a train ticket for Toronto, changed his appearance, and "disappeared" for three months. Then he began a new life as a construction laborer, eventually establishing himself as a concrete strength tester in Lyndhurst.

After a decade and half in his new profession, Henry returned to his former employer with a cashier's check for the amount of money that had been missing. It was never cashed.

Mr. Starr, the company founder, had discovered a week after Henry's disappearance that his son and the bookkeeper had taken the money. The affair was hushed up to protect the Starrs' business reputation and funds quietly restored through the sale of a family farm. Mr. Starr had tried to locate Henry to say he need not fear prosecution, but even after hiring a private detective, he could not find the missing account manager. Unaware of any of this, Henry hovered invisibly in the area, cut off from his family and a once promising career.

At home from Archer that first Christmas, Marian became his advocate within the family. Ethel, of course, accepted him back with open arms, but others remained distant, even Nana. Surely, they thought, he could have communicated with one of them in all these years. But Henry was a stern individualist and wished no shame to come to the family from his affairs. He would not make contact until his name was clear. And there'd been some split between him and his mother, Nana, years ago, when he moved out on his own. Mother would never speak of it.

During the years he was missing, Henry "Brickman" lived in a small boarding house run by a Catholic order. Understood by his coworkers to be a misanthropic recluse, he blended into the background of others' lives. Marian saw in his history a trajectory she might follow herself unless she took drastic action, for Henry had let himself be defined by the people around him.

When she returned to Baltimore in January, she told Dr. Royal she would work as promised in the Fit Female Project, but she wanted a larger role in the laboratory operation. She would coach, but she also wanted to work as a scientist.

"So, you want to become a medical technologist," her sponsor asserted.

Mid wondered, "What does a medical technologist do?"

"Hospitals are finding they can't operate without their own labs to test for diseases. Nor are individual doctors able to keep up with what can be learned about a patient's condition from sophisticated measurements of blood cells, antibodies, bacteria. MT's must undergo rigorous training, but they can identify the causes underlying symptoms a doctor observes. They are paid well, and it's a field open to women."

"Is it better than being a nurse, like you were in the war?"

"Nurses do wonderful work, but they take orders. Medical technologists may not be authorized to declare what a patient's illness is but they can present so much information that the case is clear. If it were me, if I were young, it's what I would study."

So, Mid began to look at the college courses that would qualify her for advanced study in the field, pleased to think that one day, in an orderly laboratory full of sophisticated equipment, she would be an important figure in a large hospital's operation. She might even find herself recruited to set up a new lab on the the other side of the globe, her destiny to spread good health in regions that had never known it.

Marian's work for Dr. Royal later led, in the summer between her sophomore and junior years, to a position at St. Anne's Hospital in Passaic. She labored without salary, of course: paying jobs in those days went to men, as the Depression wore on. But she was building a professional résumé, and the lab's director, Dr. Thomas Kerr, had commended her on several occasions. Now her skills were truly being tested, as her uncle's future was in question.

Another life hung in the balance that July. Her childhood friend and one time suitor, Tony Giordano, had disappeared in Spain. His letters had stopped abruptly. The International Brigade, in which Tony originally served, withdrew from the conflict. Then Tony was reported missing. His family had contacted the Red Cross, hoping to learn of his whereabouts.

Mid focused the microscope on the slide, praying for negative results. She did not want her uncle to have the disease that would do what he had always feared: shame his family.

She pushed away from the desk and breathed a sigh of relief: Uncle Henry did not have syphilis. Now if they would just hear from Bill.

Chapter 22: Stitches

Bill had volunteered to travel to China with a missionary party sponsored by a consortium of churches, including the one Father attended. Some Americans saw the ongoing civil war there and the Japanese occupation of portions of the country as an opportunity, offering the hope of Christianity to people who had never heard the good news of the Gospel.

Father hated the idea, because Bill was having to drop out of school for a year. But the man leading the group was a good friend of his and had been twice before to this area, and he had promised to keep Bill close. The rest of his family felt it was irresponsible to undertake such an expedition when many in America needed help.

"You could witness to the Negroes in Harlem," Mid told him one evening as they gathered around the radio and listened to disturbing news from Europe.

Alice, who was attracted to the new young priest at Holy Trinity Episcopal, said, "You could be a preacher, go to seminary and live right here in Rutherford."

"I feel *this* call," Bill said simply. Mother dabbed her eyes with a handkerchief.

Mid put down her knitting and looked hard at him. Was that enough for loved ones?

At first his group had been operating safely in central China, but then the Japanese took control of Shanghai and Nanjing. Bill's correspondence began to be censored by the occupiers, and the family couldn't tell whether their own letters were reaching him. It had been several months since they'd heard from him.

While Mid was spending her days at St. Anne's, her mother worried about her brother's health and her children's welfare. John had dropped out of college to work at Townbank the year before, marrying a young woman he had met when he was a counselor at a summer camp in the Adirondacks. While they didn't elope, Father was angered at this second occasion when one of his children had acted against his advice--and this time a son. The young couple were busy trying to make ends meet with a child already on the way, so Mid seldom saw them.

Ella, now mother of an infant boy, was still in Maine. Her husband sometimes had to work extra hours as a hod carrier for a construction company, and her letters to Mid were infrequent.

The youngest Lacy sister had found she was an athlete and, idolizing Helen Wills Moody, filled her after-school hours with tennis practice. This week she was participating in a tennis clinic, and Mid felt she been closer to Alice when she was at Archer and writing every week.

And, as if Mother didn't have enough to worry about, Father was preparing for a month long business trip to South America at the end of July. It seemed he had automatically assumed the reliable, self-possessed middle child would take his place as the stable center of family life, comforting Mother and making sure the house ran smoothly.

Mother was so distressed about Bill that she even considered going back to Franes Border, "Rutherford's own" clairvoyant and medium. Her claim as a seer derived from a warning she gave Gerald Effingham years ago to dig up the vegetable garden behind his garage. In the middle of his potatoes he found--or so the story went--a tin box full of gold coins, buried by his great-great-uncle during the Revolutionary War. Frances said his spirit had contacted her as she huddled before her gas grate during a fierce winter storm.

Ever since, people experiencing sorrow would come to the elderly widow's tiny house in the mews behind Park Avenue, where she'd lived alone for as long as anyone could remember. They would ask for advice about family matters, seek hints of future events, pose questions about the past. With the lights down low and a teapot steaming behind her head, Frances went into some kind of trance and offered her pronouncements, sometimes in a voice decidedly not her own. Money wasn't ever discussed, but an old sugar bowl by the entrance with a few small bills already inside was difficult to ignore.

Ethel had gone to her when Henry first disappeared.

"If he's alive, he won't speak through me," the old woman cautioned.

"Just tell me *that* he's alive," Ethel begged.

Frances closed her eyes, her lips slightly parted as she concentrated. After a silence long enough that Ethel's hopes almost disappeared, the medium shook herself awake. "He's not . . . gone. He's close . . by. He doesn't want to be found yet." Ethel didn't quite believe her, but couldn't disbelieve her either. And now, so many years later, what Frances had said seemed to be true. Henry had been in Lyndhurst all the time. But Ethel had gone to the medium without telling Curtis or Nana and was embarrassed when they'd found out. Could she go back?

Mid, like her father and the scientist she was becoming, relied on the rational mind and conventional institutions to locate her brother. However, she increasingly experienced a feeling of disconnection from family and friends: two important men in her life were overseas, where she couldn't communicate with them; and two others-- her brother and brother-in-law--were taken away in marriage. In two weeks her father would be south of the equator.

Every few months, though, she received a post card from Sydney Stuart, often from a different place: New York City, Missouri, Brazil. He did no more than draw attention to a theater or gallery or museum he visited, but she found it curious he bothered to write her at all.

In Rutherford she began to concentrate on her laboratory work, experimenting with variations on the medium they used in cell and tissue growth. She was curious about how small changes in PH or viscosity were tolerated by some micro-organisms but not others. She did not fool herself that her efforts would cure her uncle's recurring headaches, muscle pains, and loss of appetite; but accounts of medical breakthrough at other labs inspired her.

She was inspired also by Sam. Well, officially, Dr. Samuel Bridges, the young intern at St. Anne's who had seemed more than casually interested in a college student.

"You must have done this work before," he commented when he was being escorted around the building by the hospital director. She found him, for a graduate of Hopkins, unexpectedly down-to-earth, not at all like the more polished--and cynical--men she had met through Glenna.

"I've been in a research project at Archer--that's where I'm in school--for almost two years now." She smiled. "I feel at home with test tubes and petri dishes."

"I never went over to Archer when I was in Baltimore. I wish I had, though." He seemed to be recalling some specific omission. "My sister should talk to you about your study. She wants to devote herself to poetry, a profession that never comes with a salary."

"There are famous women writers, though, like Emily Dickinson and . . . "

"Christina Rossetti, yes. I admire her verse, but neither one ever married."

Marian thought of her mother and her association with Dr. Paterson, by now a quite famous poet. He was asked to read and lecture at home and abroad.

And he was her mother's friend in part because Ethel Woodruff Lacy, too, composed poems.

"Well, if it's your sister's choice, you should support her."

"Hmm. And the truth is, she has independent means. I, of course, must provide for the family I hope one day to have." He smiled and followed the director out the door. Mid wondered later if he might somehow be that tall handsome officer she had imagined meeting in some busy urban hospital-- perhaps Bombay, or Shanghai, or New York City. "A terrible train crash!" the British (oops--American) officer announces; there are dozens--perhaps hundreds of victims. He needs a nurse. Well, a medical technologist.

Before any such scene occurred in the future, there were more immediate and mundane tasks to attend to in the present, like knitting the sweater vest Mrs. Giordano had requested for her son and a weekend cleaning up at Greenwood Lake. Father wanted to be sure she understood what needed to be done at Camp Robin as well as on Ridge Road while he was away.

"I know Tony's fine," his mother had said, leaning on the fence that separated their two back yards. The look on her neighbor's face lacked the confidence of the words she uttered. "But they must have him as prisoner of war. And those poor men don't get the clothes they need."

"Of course, Mrs. Giordano, I'll make the vest. But I bet he'll be home before it's done, packaged up, and ready for shipping." She thought of the gaunt, vacant eyed young man she'd seen in Close Hall two years earlier and wasn't so confident herself.

"Do you, dear? Oh, I hope so."

Mid had been the best knitters of the three sisters, so the simple vest pattern was no challenge compared to some of the circular knitting, double knitting, and decorative stitches she was experimenting with this summer--still under Nana's supervision, of course.

She'd learned early how to daydream at the right parts of the process, counting stitches when it was crucial but letting her fingers have their way in those operations that had become mechanical. This evening she imagined herself in Frances Border's little house, seeing visions of Tony in Spain, of Bill in China, or of Samuel Bridges in Baltimore. Wait a minute! Was that Sydney at Greenwood Lake?

Chapter 23: Landings

On her way up to bed, Mid found Mother at her writing desk on the second floor, a book open on the drop down panel. She was looking out in space, though. Some nagging concern might have drawn her away from whatever she had been reading.

"Mid," she said absently, as if surprised to see her daughter here.

What the family called "Mother's study" was more of an alcove in the hall by the front stairs of the Ridge Road house. There was a tiny square of window over the porch behind the landing, and this space was brightly lit in the late afternoon.

"Yes, Mother?" Mid paused at the bottom of the stairs. She and Alice still shared a room on the third floor. Nana and Grandpa slept in separate rooms on this floor. And the boy's room was left for guests after Ella married and Bill took her third floor bedroom.

"Do you think I should . . . would it be appropriate for me to go . . . away for a time. Time to . . . take care of some things."

Mid didn't understand. "Away? You mean on a trip? Where would you go? For heaven's sake, you're not going to China are you?"

"China? Oh, to find Bill." She sighed. "No, no I couldn't do that. I just meant, maybe to Brooklyn, back where Nana and I used to live."

Mid sat down in the small bentwood rocker across from Mother. This corner was where Ethel wrote letters and made her daily journal entries in a precise, classic hand. Over the years she had filled nearly a dozen, handsome, leather bound volumes that had their places in a row of treasured books on the narrow top of the desk.

"Brooklyn? Whatever for, Mother? Father goes away in another week. Alice and I need you here, especially if Grandpa has another . . . has another lapse." He'd suffered several brief blackouts since Christmas this year, fortunately when others were present and he was sitting down. Once it happened at the dining room table; another time he was reading the paper in the living room. He just froze, his eyes glazing over. When he recovered, it was just like waking up. He would admit only to "dozing," but Father was concerned.

"Oh, Mid, you're here, and so much more . . . steady than I am."

"I don't see how that matters. What would you be doing in Brooklyn? Were you going to take Nana with you, looking at where you used to live?" She also wondered if this had something to do with Henry and his estrangement from Nana, a connection to some earlier event.

"No. I would go alone." She sighed again. "I want, really, to write more. Here, look at this." She closed the book and opened a manila folder that lay beneath it. Inside was a stack of papers. She took the top one, scanned it for a moment, then handed it to Mid.

It was a business letter, and the embossed letterhead read "*Poet Magazine.*" Below that was printed, "The Goal of this magazine is to have an Open Door." Mid looked down to the bottom of the page, where the author's name was printed, the initials, "HM," scrawled above it.

> *We are pleased to accept your poem, "Beads," for publication in our magazine. Your strong sense of poetic line and the clean, simple images have impressed us once more. Please continue to think of Poet Magazine as a place where your work might appear.*

There was another paragraph about the magazine's mission not to be bound to any one literary style and always to be seeking new voices for it pages.

"This is very nice, Mother. I didn't know you were interested in being published."

Mid had learned about the business of writing from her second English course at Archer, a survey of American literature. Mark Twain's effective promotional skills had been contrasted with Emily Dickinson's commitment to obscurity.

"Oh, I've been published, for a number of years. But it's been one poem at a time, months apart or even years. There's never enough time to put . . . to put together a longer work." She gestured at the row of books on the secretary's narrow top. Mid had looked at some of the titles--*Aurora Leigh, Maud, Goblin Market*--but had never read a single book.

"Oh, so you want to go somewhere for a few days to . . . to wrap up a collection."

168

Mid's idea of such a plan derived from the many lab reports she'd prepared for Dr. Royal in the last two years, usually at the end of a semester. With all the data tabulated and the initial proposal in front of her, she would spend a weekend putting it all in its final form.

Ethel smiled. "Well, a collection, yes, though really more of a single, large work. And it would take . . . more than a few days."

"Well, I suppose we could manage for a week, as long as we knew where you were. We could call if there were an emergency." Mid imagined her mother's figure receding in the distance as her father's had for so many years on his way to catch the train.

Mother took back the letter and put it away inside the folder. She rose to switch off the light. "I'll let you know what I decide."

Mid was uncomfortable leaving the matter in this unresolved state. "Of course, I still have to go to work every day. And Alice is out a lot for tennis. She says she wants to help with a summer program at Holy Trinity that begins in about ten days. Did she talk to you about that?"

"Oh, yes. I think that's fine. Father James seems like such a nice young man. And the Nelsons, across the street go there. It's a good congregation."

Mid thought a bit more, looking down at her feet, which suddenly seemed as if they weren't her own but someone else's, an older and more mature person's. "You have talked to Father about it, of course?"

"Certainly . . . certainly, I will . . . before he goes." She pushed the desk cover up and turned the little key at the top. She was not actually locking the desk, as the key remained in place. But it had always been understood that Mother kept her most important papers here, and no one would have thought of looking at what was inside.

When Ella married Ax, Father had proposed turning the boys' bedroom into a library, a spacious, bright room where Mother could read and write with minimal interruption. "We could put shelves along this wall," he'd said, gesturing. "We're getting some new desks at the office. I might purchase one of the old ones--still solid, just needs refinishing--and you'd have places for everything."

Mother had looked at the memorabilia in a book case between the windows, the two beds that had come from his Grandpa's upstate home, a dresser they'd bought from a neighbor transferred to an overseas branch. "No, I'd prefer to leave it for our children, when any of them comes to visit. We'll want room for grandchildren, you know."

"But there's an extra bed in Bill's room, and, well, we won't always have other family members here. You don't have to be perched on the landing in that little bit of space."

Mid recalled that exchange as she mounted the steps. Her mother was involved in a much bigger project than she'd ever imagined: writing a book. And not a book of poems, apparently, but a book of poetry. What was her subject? Was it a historical tale, a romance from the Middle Ages, perhaps? Could it be a more contemporary portrait--of a woman, say, who becomes a nurse and takes care of wounded soldiers in a field hospital far from home?

She had always known her mother as a household manager seeing a husband off to work each day; making sure meals were prepared, laundry done, carpets cleaned; taking care of her mother and father-in-law. She would know nothing of modern day adventurers pushing back the frontiers of knowledge at the far ends of the earth.

When Mid reached the door of her room, she stood completely still. Could it be that Mother was writing about herself, a woman with five children (at one time six; but an infant had died in her first year)? Would her poetry make it clear that a woman with great ability had been trapped in a far too conventional life?

After all, thought Mid, Ethel Woodruff Lacy was friends with Dr. Patrick Paterson, whose fame was international. And she was corresponding with the editor of an important literary magazine, eager to publish her work and to encourage more submissions.

She recalled how, some summers ago, the Stuarts had been willing to come to a picnic at Smelters' Point on Greenwood Lake. Mid had assumed they were being polite or couldn't find an easy way to decline. But perhaps they'd been impressed with the person who'd drawn them to her with elegant writing and gentle wit.

Could it be that Mid's mother was a woman composing a work of literature that one day might rest on library shelves beside volumes written by Christina Rossetti, Alfred Lord Tennyson, and Elizabeth Barrett Browning?

Alice came into their room when Mid was already in bed reading a technical journal. Sam had referred her to an article on hemagglutination inhibitions and new research that might affect the lab procedures she was using.

"You're out late," Mid observed as Alice was putting away her tennis racket and looking through her closet for clothes to wear the next day.

"I went to an evening prayer service at Trinity, after my last tennis session. Some of the other girls invited me."

"Um-hm. Do you like that church, or is it the priest? What's his name?"

"Father James Scott, but . . . " She giggled a bit. "He's not old enough to be a father. Or at least not my father!"

"They can marry in that church, can't they? Priests?"

"Oh, yes. It's not like in the Catholic church. Most of the Episcopal priests have families, the same as in Presbyterians. They just wear the dark shirt and white collar that the Catholics do."

Mid closed her journal, but kept a finger on the page she was reading. She turned on her side, cocking her arm at the elbow so she could raise her head and look directly at her sister.

"Alice, let me ask you something. I've never mentioned it before."

Alice sat on the bed and eyed her cautiously. "Okay."

"Do you remember that summer on Greenwood Lake. I was still in high school, and Mother invited the Stuart family for a picnic. It was when Bill . . . um, almost drowned, and that young man, Sydney, pulled him out of the water. He and Stephen, the ferry master's son, had swiped a canoe and tipped over."

"Sure. That was when Ax proposed to Ella. Father was so mad!"

"Hm. I'd forgotten that it was the same time. But it's worked out well . . . at least so far. Ax is supporting his family."

Again Alice giggled. "I remember that you and I had been spying on the Stuarts that night, when Bill . . . went under. And we watched . . . well, we heard; it was so dark we couldn't really see--the younger Stuart brother. What was his name? He was singing out on the dock. Such a beautiful voice he had!"

"Yes. Bartholomew. At first I thought he was a girl, his singing was so delicate. He's been on the radio since then. But it's his brother, Sydney, I wanted to ask about."

Alice got up and went over to the vanity they shared. Sitting on the bench, she began brushing her hair, sometimes glancing up at Mid's reflection as she turned to draw out one side.

"He was the older brother, wasn't he? Didn't you write once that you saw him at Archer? That you went to a play with him?"

"*Lost Horizons*, yes. Well, I thought of him all of a sudden because . . . because I think he was--or is, I guess--Episcopalian. His family, in Providence, is very active in that church. And in society, of course. They're rather well off."

"We never did see them at the lake after that. They must have stayed busy up north."

"Or in other places. He travels . . . they all travel a lot. The family has property, even overseas, as I remember. And somewhere in the Midwest, maybe Missouri."

"Do you know Father James showed me a big story in some church publication about the shanty towns out there, along that big highway that goes to California. It was in St. Louis, I think, where the Mississippi River had gotten out of its banks. And people had their makeshift shelters flooded and had nowhere to go. It was a few years ago, but they haven't rebuilt those areas."

"Hmm. I was in St. Louis, remember, with Father one winter. We didn't see anything like that, though."

"Well, the pictures were pretty sad. People standing in the mud where their shacks had been, all their belongings swept away. And back here, why, we're just fine! We haven't felt the Depression the way some people have. Father James thinks we should do more, those of us who have been fortunate, those whom God has blessed."

"Yes, I see." Mid paused. The Lacys didn't generally speak about blessings coming from above: God helps those who help themselves. Father, who went to his own church in Newark, knew Jesus was his Savior but also insisted that he alone was responsible for taking care of his family. Bill was convinced he was being called to save souls, not improve the living conditions of the less fortunate. The poor we will always have with us, but they are not us.

Mid went on. "Anyway, that's what I was thinking, about the Stuarts, I mean. Did you . . . uh . . . did Sydney, the older brother, did he ever flirt with you that summer? I was just remembering, maybe he liked you. And I just wondered if you ever heard from him afterwards."

Alice kept brushing her hair but didn't say anything for a moment. "Oh, I never heard from him, but I did . . . I believe he might have paid me . . . more attention than was proper, given that I was pretty young and we had just met."

Mid waited to see if she would say more. But Alice gave a last series of energetic brush stokes and then clicked off the little lamp by the dressing table. Returning to her bed and slipping under the sheet, she said, "Mother says there are other college students at St. Anne's this summer. Do you fancy any of them?"

"Oh, my! Well, there's certainly no line of gentlemen callers, flowers in hand, marching down Ridge Road to knock on my door." She put her magazine on the little table by her bed and reached up to turn off the lamp. "In fact, boys in general don't seem interested in me."

This time Alice turned on her side and propped her head on one hand. "Now that's silly. Tony wanted to snap you up, as I remember, even when he was in high school. And you've talked about boys you've met from Hopkins. You're just too picky, Mid. You want some . . . some really smart man, a professor or a scientist. Boys don't go for girls who are too intelligent."

"Hummf." Mid rolled over away from Alice. "I'm not *that* smart!"

But as they settled toward sleep, she began to wonder: was she waiting for some larger than life figure who made the boys she'd grown up with and dated at Archer seem ordinary? She thought about Glenna and all the would-be suitors she had dismissed as beneath her notice.

Well, in her case they were. Glenna had defied her own predictions and applied to medical school at Columbia. Her record was so good that she had been accepted early and she would start in the fall. Mid believed her former roommate had left a trail of broken hearts behind her at Archer and would do so again in the city.

Had her friend's self-confidence--perhaps arrogance--sloughed off onto Mid? Mid thought about the potential suitors she had known. She realized she had always thought of Tony, the boy next door, as too familiar, too much a part of home. She'd been close to Tim Jensen for a few weeks; but when, for thirty minutes, he shared a bed with

Glenna, she saw him as another weak victim, not a genuine social revolutionary.

The men she found attractive were almost by definition out of reach. Sydney was distant in manner, social standing, and interests. She liked Sam, but, a young doctor whose residence could be anywhere and his practice anywhere else, he probably had high ambitions. And he would only be in Mid's vicinity for another six weeks before she went back to Archer.

There had been acquaintances, to be sure: Rutherford boys and Hopkins students, friends of men dating other Archer girls, cousins twice or thrice removed. But, for some reason, she'd never looked on them as romantic possibilities. Was she pushing away potential lovers before they even appeared on the horizon? Were they all around her but obscured by dreams of a heroic mate in an exotic, faraway landscape?

That funny boy in St. Louis? She didn't even know his name, the one who said he would be another Einstein. He told her that Mark Twain's "Platonic Sweetheart" had been more real to the author than women in his own life. They were . . . what ? "Living spirits, not shadows . . . immortal and indestructible." Was she turning away flesh and blood men in the real world for figures in a dream?

She'd once been put into a dream herself, of course, by Dr. Paterson's poem, an angel rising to heaven. Could she now connect only to another creature woven from fantasies? Or perhaps she was not yet really a grown person, just a immature idea of woman incubating in some gigantic Petri dish in a land of giants.

Her last thought, before she finally fell asleep, was that she might be waiting for an ideal man in order to avoid accepting any man.

At the lake that weekend, Mid tried not to look up the shore for signs the Stuart house was occupied, concentrating instead on her father's detailed directions. Even if someone were there, she realized, it was more likely to be one of the local family that looked after the property for the owners, checking that no animals had gotten inside the cottage or that no storms had damaged the structure. Sometimes, too, maintenance would be under way that required oversight.

"I'm reconnecting all the appliances," her father said, itemizing instructions as he worked by marking a list in his pocket notebook. "It's safest to unplug everything when you go."

Mid had seen him do this many times, but she made a notation on her clipboard. Carrying a clipboard was a habit she'd picked up working for Dr. Royal and carried forward to the lab at St. Anne's. It strengthened the reputation she'd already earned for attention to detail and steady application. Today she saw it drawing her closer to her father.

"We want the breeze when we're here, of course, but I will double check all the window locks before I leave."

She made another entry row under the "tasks" column, but, glancing at him, she thought there was more tension in his face than appropriate for this project. She wondered if he might want to talk about something other than mechanical chores.

John had always been the one taken into Father's confidence, the oldest son and probably the most gifted. While Ethel heard his worries, most of the time she reassured him that all would be well, that he was so conscientious nothing could be neglected. It was an arrangement of responsibilities that, in the end, suited them both. Today, however, Mid wondered if Mother had told him of her desire to go away for a time to write.

"You know, I'd really like to retire somewhere near here. Build a more substantial house, buy some more land, establish a substantial vegetable garden. We could in put flower beds, both where the sun is good, but also some shade gardens."

Mid didn't see her mother digging in this rocky soil or spending cold winters away from the comforts of Ridge Road. In recent years, she did less and less with the perennials she'd planted long ago next to the Giordano's yard.

"I'd love to be here more, too," Mid said, "ice skating, canoeing, sailing. Of course, I still plan to work."

"Well, or raise a family." This was the scenario he kept for Alice and Mid, both maintaining households close enough to help their parents as he and Ethel had done for Grandpa and Nana. (Ella was supposed to have done so as well.) Mid's career as a medical technologist was to him a holding action until real life began. Mid admitted to herself that sometimes that scenario was more believable than one she created around an imagined professional career.

She observed, "Retirement's a long way off, though." She didn't know his exact age, but assumed he was not much older than 50.

"Not so far, especially if . . . if our firm's current plans go as we."

"Oh?"

They were moving into the two bedrooms (one had been added last summer), checking the closets for moths in the clothes stored there and scanning the floors for mice droppings.

"I'm not overly optimistic, but we're certain there are substantial new opportunities overseas. A lot of companies are developing branches in South and Latin America, and we're going to do the same. It's true that the Germans have established themselves in many places, but we think they're over extended. And the other countries of Europe are not going to let them take over. Still, we know there are risks . . . risks."

Mid wondered at his trailing off. "I keep reading that their military is growing, that their army is huge and that they have all sorts of new weapons."

He backed out of a closet and stood more erect. "They won't risk war. There's too much at stake. England and France are strong, and the Russians won't let them expand in their direction. While the Old World competes against each other, it's time for America to profit."

"Professor Royal says there will also be new places in the medical field overseas."

They had come back into the living room, and Mid began folding the sheets they had pulled from the furniture. They would be neatly put away in a hall cupboard Father had built. When they left for winter, he covered everything he could, as dust made its way through the thin clapboard walls and around the windows.

"You did blood tests on Uncle Henry, didn't you?" Father asked, pausing in his itemization of tasks. "Because he's not been well." After his reappearance, Henry had continued with the concrete company in Lyndhurst, rising as a slump tester to a good position as an engineer.

"Everything came out negative. We . . .um, the doctors can't find a cause for his tiredness, the loss of weight." Mid felt the spartan lifestyle he'd perfected as Henry Brickman might be responsible. It included so few pleasures.

"We should shake out those blankets and the sheets."

She went through the kitchen and out the back door with her armload of covers. In the yard she looked north and thought she did see a car. It was hard to tell at this distance, but it might be a Packard.

When she came back in, Father said. "Be sure that the food cans are tightly sealed. And take home anything that might be perishable." He was opening cabinets above the sink and testing the metal lids on floor, sugar, and coffee tins. "I always worry when we're away. It's almost as if there are gaps in Camp Robin's history we don't know about, times where none of us is here but the cabin gets warmer, then colder; rain and snow fall; winds blow across the lake."

Marian chuckled. "Ooh, and there could be ghosts within these walls, remembering times when there were no Lacys here. Or even earlier, when no Lacys had even arrived at Nantucket, and Indians roamed the hills."

"Hmph." Father was not given to fancy, which accounted in part for his lack of interest in the poetry his wife read and loved..

She stepped into the hall and began stacking the folded items in the cupboard.

Father said, "I'm worried about Mother. She seems so . . . so preoccupied."

"Well, we all worry about Bill. Grandpa and Uncle Henry aren't well. And Tony. You know how upset Mrs. Giordano is." She sighed, thinking about how little she'd done on the sweater vest so far. "There are wars, it seems, everywhere."

Mid's father turned to her and started to say something, but stopped. She raised her eyebrows and waited, scanning his face. He looked hard at her for what seemed a long time and then stepped over to take both her hands in his. She almost pulled away.

Then he said slowly and solemnly, "I want you to promise me something, Marian." While Curtis was a calm man who seldom showed emotion, he was not always a serious man. But at that moment he was as intense as the time he rushed back from Manhattan to tend to his mother, who had collapsed on the porch at Ridge Road.

"Don't you ever . . . ever . . . let yourself become attached to a soldier."

After a long pause, she asked, "Do you mean like Tony""

He paused. "Yes, like him . . . but anyone who enlists or is called up or talks about volunteering. Do not become attached."

"Yes, Father. I understand . . . what it is you want. Of course, I've never been serious about Tony. I mean he's a nice boy and everything, but . . . "

He continued to hold her hands. "Just promise."

"I . . . I promise."

"Let's look at the toolshed," Father announced, dropped her hands, and turned toward the back, as if that were the logical conclusion to this strange oath taking. And soon they had returned to the rhythm of chore identified, chore recorded.

Still, Mid wondered, as she made her notes on the clipboard and studied Father's directions, what had inspired this unexpected demand? It would be three years before she learned, but when she heard that story she tried to commit herself again to honoring his request. Sadly, it was too late. Right now she decided she could avoid an attachment to anyone who might go off to war; but she didn't give up her own conviction that she could go to places of conflict as part of some medical or scientific team.

Hiking along the lakeshore later that evening, she again imagined herself in some distant land performing tasks only men had done previously. When, in her mind's eye, a distinguished visiting physician asked how she'd come to such a place, she didn't realize she was hearing the voice of someone in Northern New Jersey.

"Wherever did you come from?" asked Sydney Stuart.

Chapter 26: Backing

Marian looked up to find a man who--she'd thought--was hundreds of miles away in Rhode Island, or perhaps even farther at one of his overseas estates.

"Sydney! Or, Mr. Stuart. What a . . . surprise to see you . . . here."

Without turning, he gestured, smiling, over his shoulder. "Well, that *is* our cottage." She realized she'd walked to within a hundred yards of the Stuart house. "And we do come here from time to time. But we saw no signs of life at your cabin when we arrived two days ago."

"Oh, we just got in this afternoon. My father's going away on business soon, and I'm to keep tabs on . . . on Camp Robin."

"I'm sure you're the right person for the job. You're home for the summer?"

"Yes. I'm working at St. Anne's Hospital in Passaic. It's Catholic, but not all the staff are of that faith." She wasn't sure why she'd added that. "Anyway, they have expanded their clinical laboratory, and I'm learning new techniques as a summer . . . volunteer."

At first she hesitated to admit she received no compensation for her labor, but then it occurred to her that the Stuarts might serve in various capacities without pay, having large incomes from property and business interests. She was unsalaried, of course, because men had their families to support, and it was understood that her father would provide for her.

"Ah, that's admirable. St. Joseph's in Providence put me on their board of governors a few years ago. A honorary post, to be sure, but sometimes my financial knowledge can be helpful. They're still recovering from a fire that destroyed the top two floors some six or eight years ago."

"So, are you at the lake for a rest? Are other family members with you?"

"Ah, . . . no, no other family members at present, but a friend . . . a person I've known for some time. She needed a chance to get away, to rest in . . . a beautiful retreat." He waved across the lake and at the hills on the other side.

"I've heard your brother on the radio, more than once."

"Yes, he's been a guest vocalist for a number of programs. but, at least so far, he's not been selected as a band's principal singer. The wheelchair, I think, makes some people nervous."

"I see." Mid wanted him to say more about his house guest. But after a pause he went on.

"And your family, how are they? You have quite a few brothers and sisters."

She gave a succinct update on parents, siblings, grandparents. Dusk was falling, and Mid knew she should return to Camp Robin soon.

"Well, it's nice to see you again," she said. "I ought to tend to Father. I think he may be getting some fishing tackle ready for the morning."

"I must return as well. The Watsons, our caretakers, are bringing a late dinner. But perhaps you and I will see each other again before you leave."

Mid noted that he didn't ask her to step up to his cottage. Nor did he include his guest in this reference to meeting again. She wondered if "she" was his age, younger, or older.

Approaching Camp Robin, she recalled the woman Sydney had left her to speak with during the intermission of *Lost Horizons* at the Hippodrome. An older woman--well, older than she had been--and certainly poised and attractive, well-dressed and sophisticated. Sydney's girl in that port, she had concluded. She was not even that for Greenwood Lake, only a recipient of post cards sent from other ports.

She compared him to Sam Bridges, recalling the day the doctor gave her an article to read.

She had been sitting in the cafeteria with two other summer employees, students from Rutgers: Susan, on her left, was planning to teach physical hygiene in high school; and Helen, on the other side, was the daughter of an important physician at the hospital. Their eyes went wide when Dr. Bridges sat down across from them.

"Hello, Marian," he said, then looked at the other girls. "Excuse me for interrupting . . . ?"

"Oh, that's fine," Helen said, waving a hand as if to brush away their own insignificant conversation. She knew he'd gone to Johns Hopkins and assumed he and Marian would have common interests, if not a shared past.

"Um, Dr. Bridges, this is Helen, and Susan. They work with me."

"Nice to meet you. You may all be interested in this, but I brought it for Mid especially." He handed the journal to her. "There's a good article there about cell growth. It might bring you up to date on some new ideas."

Mid pulled it across the table and scanned the cover. "I . . . I'll read it. But if I have questions . . . ?" Without raising her head, she glanced coyly.

"I'll be glad to discuss it with you. Whenever they give me some free time!"

The interns joked that the hospital wanted them working around the clock." He looked at his watch. "In fact, I'm supposed to be on third floor . . . five minutes ago."

Mid accepted the inevitable teasing from her co-workers, insisting that this exchange was entirely professional. She hoped it wasn't. She hoped this was a prelude to his asking her out.

The following Sunday, as Father loaded their weekend bags into the car, she recalled again Sam's promise to speak with her--in rather clear contrast to Sydney the other day. She asked Father if he'd seen any of the Stuart family while they'd been here.

"I did see the Stuart son, in fact, early this morning--Sydney. I was drifting past their dock, and he came out to speak." Father had been angling for smallmouth bass with worms as bait, at dawn cruising the shoreline where old stumps provided traditionally good places to cast.

"Yes, he told me a friend was recuperating with him. I haven't seen either of them since the evening we arrived, though."

"He and I didn't talk long, but he was interested in my business in South America. Apparently, his family has holdings there."

"I think they must be quite wealthy. They have houses in different places, boats, plantations--maybe even factories."

"He's worried about the steel industry, especially if war comes."

"Didn't you say there would be no war? And if there is, surely it will be in Europe. They're the ones who have the history of conflict; the Great War was only the most recent." She'd learned in high school and at Archer about the 100 Years War, the 30 Years War, the Napoleonic wars, the Austro-Prussian War.

"Yes, there's too much at stake and the armies are too large. It would be suicidal."

Mid went back into the kitchen to get two cardboard boxes of linens they would carry home to be cleaned. While they had an old washtub with a wringer dryer here, it was much easier to have things laundered in Rutherford.

A few minutes later, she asked, "Aren't our factories making weapons and equipment to sell to England and France, our allies? Won't that help the steel industry."

"Oh, yes. That's been a boon in recent months. Apparently, though, Stuart's father fears, if we become involved, the industry could be nationalized. So they're looking to shift their investments over . . . um, to places where governments don't interfere."

"That seems a little like . . . well, not betraying your country exactly . . . but not fully standing behind it. Won't we all want to work together?"

"This is business, Marian. Companies can't operate efficiently if governments become involved. Financial backers have to look elsewhere with their money in those case."

They walked together around the cabin, checking windows from the outside. At one point he added, "Sydney is also worried about Labor after the Little Steel Strike. And I have to agree that the Unions have gained strength with U.S. Steel, the industry leader."

Mid remembered some of things Tim Jensen had explained to her about the history of the working class, the monied interests that would do anything, he claimed, to keep workers from gaining power. Tim felt our government could not be trusted to protect the working classes either. He said Marx had proven that capital is power, and that power corrupts.

"Your company doesn't have anything to do with unions, does it?"

"No. Our cleaning crew chooses not to join, and the clerical staff are happy with what we pay them, especially in these hard times. We take care of our own at Manhattan Marine." He ended the discussion as decisively as he closed the car door on Mid.

On the ride home, out of nowhere, it seemed to Mid, he told her not to mention seeing Sydney Stuart to Mother or to talk about the goals of his upcoming business trip. She started to ask why, but, seeing the fixed look on Father's face, she knew he was not going to explain.

And now, she realized, she had become keeper of secrets for both of her parents.

Chapter 27: Materialization

Back home in her own room, Marian contemplated the set of scales, handed down, according to some in the family, by John Lacy, Nantucket shopkeeper, to his son, Rowland H. Lacy, founder of the famous department store chain. The brass balances came on down the genealogical line to Curtis, who thought his middle daughter the appropriate keeper of this treasure. Tonight she weighed in the balance what father and mother had told her, imagining the bar swinging first this way, then that, as she imagined the future.

There was, she had to admit, some evidence of a schism between her parents--one thinking of leaving Rutherford to write; the other off on a South American business venture he didn't want to admit involved risk. There would be a physical separation, but would that also mean a division of minds? If so, would she be the one to maintain the connections?

Before she could decide if she should share these worries with her siblings, she confronted two different problems. First, a letter had been waiting for her on Ridge Road from Diana Tracy, her college classmate. And then Mother insisted she go see her Uncle Henry.

Diana wrote that she would be coming into Newark on a train over the weekend; and she had a three-hour layover. Could Mid possibly--please, please!--come see her for part of that time. There was a family crisis she needed to talk about with "her best friend."

Diana's career at Archer had bloomed after her uneven beginning. Poorly prepared and intimidated by more sophisticated classmates, she'd almost given up in her first term. But the Fit Female Program and Dr. Royal's attention had encouraged her to think of herself as a woman with distinctive characteristics.

That she could outperform even Ruth Montgomery and Mary Hobarts, the other two test subjects--both older and more successful academically--gave her a self-confidence that gradually spilled over into her course work. And, as Dean Dupont and Dr. Royal had predicted, Mid was a good coach, able to give and withhold help at the right times.

There was not enough time for a letter to reach Diana back home in West Virginia, so Marian sent a telegram that she would be at the station on Sunday. She sent it on her way to work the next morning, then boarded a train for Lyndhurst at the end of her day.

Mother had asked her to check on Uncle Henry because, when they'd last spoken on the telephone, his voice sounded weak and he wouldn't talk long. Ethel must have felt guilty, Mid decided: worrying so much about Bill, and thinking about poetry, she hadn't taken time to stay in touch with her reclusive brother even though she knew he had health problems.

Mid had visited Uncle Henry at Waypoint House before, and the lobby always depressed her: worn floors, aging furniture, fading pictures of Christ and various suffering martyrs on the walls. She knew residents could decorate their own rooms, but they couldn't remove the crucifix above the bed or the rosaries on the bedside table. She wouldn't want to live there.

There was always an elderly "Porter" stationed at the front desk, a retired layperson given the post in appreciation for long service to the Benedictine Order that ran the "single Christian gentleman's boarding house." Mid felt porters were chosen for sullen manner and ability to discourage visitors.

Today, reading from the desk name plane, she tried to be outgoing and bright. "Hello, Mr. Holder. I'm here to see Mr. Brickman."

Henry had decided it would be awkward to change his name at this residence, having been here so long, but he had gradually begun to use "Woodruff" in other places.

Mr. Holder said, without moving, "I can ring him. You are . . . "

"I'm his niece, Marian. I've been here before."

He studied her face, not even glancing at the intercom on the counter. "And your business would be?"

"It's personal, family. He's my uncle, as I said."

He looked back at the grid of wooden mailboxes behind him, as if the little cubicle with his name on it might be a passageway to Mr. Brickman's room. Mid feared his room would be nearly as sparse at that empty space. Finally, Mr. Holder said, "I'll see if he's available."

As he reached for the crank on the intercom, the elevator beside the front desk opened, revealing another aging figure pulling up the metal lever that opened and closed the doors. He stood to one side to reveal Uncle Henry.

She recalled receiving Tony Giordano at Close Hall two years earlier. He'd had a blank look on his face months after being knocked senseless by an explosion in Spain. Her uncle had a similar look now.

He smiled to see her, however, but said nothing. Taking him by the elbow she escorted him to the parlor. "Uncle Henry, it's so good to see you. Mother was worried that she hadn't heard from you. And you wouldn't say much over the phone."

Her mother's complaint was not completely fair. Because of the cost of long distance, even between neighboring cities, no one in the family would talk long on the phone. But Henry explained patiently that he'd been busy with his regular routine: work and reading. He loved historical novels, especially those, like *Ivanhoe*, set in the Middle Ages.

Pressed, Henry insisted that he was at least no worse than he'd been when Mid had taken his blood at St. Anne's. "I'm not getting any younger, Marian. What I've been feeling may just be age." Henry was older than Ethel, but he claimed "never to have been sick a day" in his life.

"Perhaps you need to get out more, go walking, for instance. Mother wishes you'd come to dinner or

197

just to visit. Or you could go with me into the city one day."

They'd gone several times the previous summers, to walk past shops and have lunch in Central Park. Henry had a typical dreamy look, though, as if focusing on another landscape, perhaps from memory. "Do you know what purgatory is?" he asked.

She looked around the room, as if there were an illustration that made him ask. She thought about what she'd been told by some of her fellow workers at St. Anne's. "Well, according to Catholics, isn't it a place of purification, while you wait to get into heaven?"

"Yes. You're not still here on earth, but you're not with God in heaven either. I used to feel that's where I was . . . well, there or in limbo, waiting to descend the rest of the way into the realm of the damned. All those years after the . . . the incident, I was waiting to be called up or sent down, to move on to the final state."

"Well, you were been called up two years ago; you're here."

"That's what I thought. I was so relieved to erase the mark of 'sin' from the past . . . "

"Sin?" Mid interrupted him. "You hadn't done anything wrong! Two other men in the company framed you; they said that you were a criminal. But it wasn't true."

Henry sighed, again gazing across the room as if they were not confined by the plain walls of this old room, the heavy drapes darkening even a sunny summer day. "It's hard to explain, Marian. When you've lived for a long, long time, convinced that everyone thinks of you in a certain way--as . . . as an embezzler, or a forger, or a rash young man--it isn't so easy to shrug it off and pick up your life where you'd left it."

She was silent, feeling sorry for him. Later she would learn there was more to his belief that he'd sinned and feel even greater pity for how fate had dealt with such a dear man.

Mid's picture of purgatory placed it near hell, across a river of limbo. There was a visible reminder of how close the souls on hold still were to eternal fire. Also within view, however, was heaven, tantalizingly present but, until the right moment, unattainable. Poor Uncle Henry!

But Mid felt suspended, too. She'd been an angel rising to heaven for nearly a decade, a girl who, in a poem, died and drifted away from earth. Ever since she'd learned about the poetic version of her childhood self, it seemed as if others didn't recognize her as a living, breathing resident of earth. She was someone's experiment, an insubstantial area into which a more powerful figure might pour his own desires.

Tony wanted someone to hear his war stories; Tim wanted a fellow soldier in the class war; Sydney wanted one more girl in one more port. How could she appear before them as a material woman, a female whose presence would change all those around her, make them different because she was in their world?

Dr. Sam Bridges, she thought to herself: I'm going to put myself someplace at St. Anne's where he has literally to run into me. I'm getting out of my Petri dish as a fully formed organism, a fit female to be reckoned with, a woman to be . . . a sweetheart . . . to be kissed.

Chapter 28: Rescues

When Mid pulled open the front screen door at the house on Ridge Road, Alice appeared in front of her and proclaimed, "Tony's been found!"

Mid had trouble shifting her thoughts from an uncle who seemed lost to the boy next door who had been found. The look on her face must have been blank, as Alice grabbed her by her elbows and leaned close to explain. "He's alive. He's coming home." She pulled Mid with her into the living room where she saw Mother sitting with a beaming Mrs. Giordano.

Finally, she took in what was happening. "Tony's alive? Where? In Spain?"

"Yes, yes," answered Alice. "Mrs. Giordano, here, is telling everything to Mother. It's all so exciting."

Tony's mother alternately laughed and cried as she recounted what she'd already told her family: her son was in a prisoner of war camp near Gandesa, but the Red Cross had seen him, found him to be healthy (if a bit undernourished), and were pleading for his speedy release and repatriation. Older siblings and other relatives would be gathering next door the following evening to celebrate the news and plan his homecoming.

"Isn't this wonderful?" Ethel asked Mid, who quickly agreed. But she also saw a look of strain beneath Mother's smile. Mid was sure this good news was making Mother think of her own son: the world had remained silent about the Lacy boy far from home. Still, they couldn't let their worries affect the Giordanos' happiness.

In the coming weeks they would learn how lucky Tony had been. Franco held foreign and domestic political prisoners long beyond the end of conflict. And the Red Cross and other relief agencies gained the release of only a tiny percentage of them. Why they freed this American was never understood, as all evidence showed he had hardly been an unarmed combatant with the International Brigade.

At that time, Mid didn't think much about what Tony would be like when he finally returned home, a date that remained uncertain for much longer than everyone hoped. After her father's strict injunction against involvement with soldiers and her own sense that Tony's teenage declaration of love was an adolescent impulse, she continued to feel her future should follow the path of her own career and that any romantic prospects would appear wherever her jobs took her.

Later that night, when the neighborhood excitement had waned, she overheard her parents talking on the front porch. The summer heat had taken many in the neighborhood outdoors.

"I worry so about Bill," Ethel was saying. "He's still a child. He should be in school."

"Of course we worry. But he's a missionary, not a soldier; that will protect him."

Marian, on her way to her room, had paused at the landing beside Mother's writing desk. She could hear the conversation below through the open window.

"I know I've asked before, Curtis, but can't your business associates, your clients, use their influence to . . . to just find out . . . "

"Ethel, there are no go-betweens inside China right now. It's war between invaders and the government. The Communists don't like either group, but still would not help an American. Those businesses that have been allowed to stay on are constantly in danger. They have to worry about their own interests. They're responsible to their investors back home."

Mid could hear Mother sigh. And her sigh had a tremor. "I would go," she told her husband, "if I could. I'd find a way to reach him . . . to speak with him."

He did not respond, but Mid intuitively concluded that, as soon as Father left for South America, Mother would go to Frances Border. And if she was told Bill was in danger, she'd do more. Mid decided she would have to go with Mother to the little house behind Park Avenue.

Determined not to give up the pursuit of her own desires, however, Mid began to look in earnest for the right opportunity at St. Anne's to engage Sam Bridges. It came just two days after she saw Diana Tracy.

At a coffee shop near the Newark station, Diana tearfully confessed her family's situation--and how it meant she would probably not be coming back to

Archer. "We're losing the farm," she said. "Daddy's been . . . cheated."

"Diana, that can't be! Didn't you inherit the land from your grandfather, and he from his father before that? I thought the Tracy family had lived in that valley forever."

"Yes, we have. Daddy thought he was just letting the coal company lease the thirty acres up in the hollow. They told him they wanted to explore for oil and gas. It wasn't supposed to be that they could take the top off our mountain."

"Wait a minute. They're going to destroy the land you're living on?"

Diana squeezed her tea bag with a spoon and set it on the saucer.

"Unless we can buy the lease back from them, which is . . . well, we simply can't. You see, the contract had all this fine print, about future rights to purchase more land unless we matched their offer. Daddy didn't understand it. And we couldn't afford a lawyer to explain it to us."

"But that's horrible and unfair! No one should . . . " Mid was about to say something about taking advantage of uneducated people. " . . . no one should should sneak things in like that, where a person wouldn't know what it meant."

She was sure Father's company wouldn't operate in such an underhanded way. She did wonder, though, about the Stuarts and their vast business operations. If they were ready to pull out of the steel industry, ignoring the national interest, would they also be the kind of people to exploit those who didn't have the means to protect themselves?

Diana went on. "My brothers want to go to work . . . in the mines . . . to earn the money to pay the company, but that would leave Daddy and Mama to run the farm all by themselves. And they're getting on." Mid knew she had three brothers, two older and one younger. Diana had told her that working the mines was dangerous.

"And that means you can't come back to Archer?"

Diana tried to smile, but her lips were quivering. "I don't think so. That's why I'm going to New York City."

Mid had a vision of her friend going into the coal company office and doing to the chief executive officer what she'd done to the feeder of pigeons on Light Street her first year at Archer.

"Who do you go to see in New York? Is that where the coal company's headquarters are?"

"No. No, that's where my uncle lives. Well, he has a house there, but he really lives in Europe, in Switzerland mostly."

"In Switzerland? Is he . . . did he leave home. I mean, West Virginia?"

"Yes, back in the '20s, before the Depression. He went to work for AT&T overseas and has been promoted, oh, lots of times. He never married, he never had to pay income tax, and he had a living allowance all those years. Daddy says, by now, he's surely a millionaire. He just comes every couple of years to check on his bankers. I haven't seen him since I was five years old."

This man, Mid realized, had stayed out of the country as things were getting worse and worse back home. He exempted himself from family obligations endured during the Depression. It was like the Stuart family, in the steel business so long as everything was favorable to them. "So you hope he'll loan you the money to keep the farm?"

"Daddy wants me to tell him to buy the farm and let us work it, see it as an investment."

"Ah. And one day the family would buy it back from him? It sounds like a good idea."

Mid recalled the images Alice had mentioned to her, of poor families flooded out of their homes along the Mississippi River. That was far away, though she had actually visited the same region with Father. Here with her now was a friend whose family might lose all they owned. What could they do? They couldn't take that big highway west and start over in California.

What would the Lacys do if they had to move from Ridge Road, Mid wondered? Well that was unthinkable. Even in these hard times Father's business was booming, John was in a good job, and Axel had proven to be resilient and resourceful--former dredger, would-be engineer, sometime hod carrier. And look at Mid herself! More than half way through college and already training to be a medical specialist who could work in any hospital in the United States or abroad.

Oddly, though, in one way, this security was disappointing. If Diana convinced her uncle to help, she would have battled unfairness and distinguished herself by surviving. Even if she had to go back to West Virginia, she would be engaged with the forces of history. She, with her brothers and sisters, would build a new life together, even if some of them had to dig coal.

Stable and reliable, on the other hand, Mid was comfortable and settled. She could imagine nothing that might destroy the structure of the Lacy family. So where was her place in the larger struggle of society?

Chapter 29: Currents

Mother didn't wait for Father to board the train in Newark before contacting Rutherford's medium. (Curtis would go first to Baltimore, where the firm had a branch office, before sailing to South America.) Fortunately, Mid overheard her talking on the phone and confronted her.

"If you're going to have the tea leaves read," she told her coldly, "I'm think I'd better be there with you." She expected resistance, as it might seem that she was prematurely stepping into Father's role as her advisor.

Ethel looked blankly at her for a moment. "Oh, I'm so glad! I'm afraid I have a tendency to let my imagination go, and you're so sensible. You can balance my . . . my dreams."

Mid didn't tell her she had her own dreams, especially after having agreed to go boating with Sam Bridges near the Great Falls of the Passaic.

Still, as she sat silently in the seer's dark living room later that week, straining to hear Mrs. Border's hoarse, low whisper, Mid wondered if what was said might apply to her rather than to other family members. She was irritated in the end to find that the prophecy offered was frustratingly vague: "Your traveler is in danger. Prepare for a change."

Of course, she couldn't be sure she had heard correctly from her vantage point. Mrs. Border told her she had to take a low easy chair in the corner during the session. "I sense your skepticism," the medium insisted. "Only those who believe they can believe shall sit with me." She meant Mid couldn't sit at the small round table draped in a white cloth, suspiciously like the ones so often pictured with a crystal ball at the center.

With their hands palm down on the surface and eyes closed, the seer and her client remained motionless and quiet for at least ten minutes. Mid cooperated to the extent of maintaining a similar stillness. Then Mrs. Border began to tremble slightly and moan. The moan increased until it became a question: "Do you have a message for Ethel?" After a long pause, a different voice answered, though the medium's lips moved to the words.

Nothing more specific than an endangered traveler and change on the way, however, was forecast that night. The effect of this vision on Mother, however--contrasting as it did with Mrs. Giordano's answered hopes--increased her nervous state in the weeks to come . . . in the end with telling effect. Still, Mid wondered if it might mean she was herself to be subject to the forces of history as Diana was. In the meantime, she launched her own bid for change, the date with Sam.

"We could have a picnic," he had suggested at the hospital cafeteria one weekday. This time as she was eating alone. "If we start early, it will be cool and we'll find a shady place."

The idea of water recreation had come up when she told him about her responsibility for the cabin in Father's absence. "It's quiet there, sometimes too

209

quiet," she explained. "When we were younger, my siblings would be there, and we always had something to do. Now, Mother is occupied in town, and my younger sister has committed herself to being the best tennis player on the school's team in the fall, so . . . ."

"So you don't think you'll be there often before you return to school. I sympathize. The director has scheduled me for at least one day every weekend, so I fear I won't be doing much sightseeing around here. And I grew up on water! My brother and I restored an old wooden skiff, the *White Cloud*, and sailed her into every nook and cranny along the Providence River."

Mid wondered if he was hinting that he'd like to boat on Greenwood Lake. Emboldened, she offered, "They say the Passaic has some pretty spots, further up river."

"Why don't we take a look, then? I believe I have this Sunday afternoon off. Shall we make it an outing?" And that weekend they were dodging barge traffic and a handful of other pleasure boats in light wind but a steady current.. She'd told her parents only that she was meeting "a friend from work."

There had been little recreational boating in the modern era along this section of the Passaic, as factories and sewage plants routinely pumped waste into the water on both sides. With a new sewer trunk built in the 1920s, however, conditions improved slightly and more hopeful residents of the area imagined a gradual restoration of natural beauty.

Sadly, this period proved only a brief interlude in the degradation of a beautiful natural waterway.

"You worked with Dr. Royal, I understand?" Sam asked once they were under way.

"I did. Well, still do. I'm a senior research assistant in the Physiology Department, keeping records and, um, preparing lab reports, project proposals."

"She's pretty important, I hear. The Fit Female Project is beginning to get attention."

"Yes. I've been involved pretty much from the beginning. A good friend is one of the subjects, and Dr. Royal asked me to coach all the young women in their exercises, their concentration, the development of endurance."

Having rejected the umbrella he offered her against the sun, she was allowing him to do the rowing. He seemed to tire quickly, however, as he pulled toward the Great Falls. She smiled to herself that Diana would not even have been perspiring at the oars. And, enjoying the summer sun on her face and remembered her own canoeing on Greenwood Lake, she was pretty sure she could do as well as he was right now. He was not particularly skilled, splashing on the backstroke and getting the oars too deep or two shallow.

"I've been wondering," Sam went on, "if I should think about pursuing a research career. The hospital . . . well, you know, you keep fixing people up, and more people come in who are sick, so you try to help them. But there are no real solutions or cures."

"Dr. Royal was a nurse, in the war, before she went back to school and began to teach and conduct research. Dr. Schure sought her out. She's very important."

He lifted the oars out of the water and let the boat drift for a few moments. "You've met her, Dr. Schure, then?"

"Of course. She comes to the lab now and then. She and Dr. Royal are very good friends, along with Miss Dupont. She's the Dean of Students."

"Ah, well, that's good. You're rubbing shoulders, it looks to me, with people who are consulted by foundation heads and corporate leaders."

"Well, I don't know about that . . . " Mid surveyed the shore, which now appeared to be moving forward as the current pulled them downriver.

"I heard their presentation at a conference on national manpower resources at Mount Sinai. There were all sorts of questions and offers . . . well, there was interest at least that might lead to more sponsors for their projects. Did you help prepare their material?"

She began to wonder if this was a date or a professional inquiry?

"Not that I'm aware. I submit reports routinely, but often don't know what happens to them." She decided to change the subject. "Would you look! The Falls are magnificent."

The river cascades seventy-seven feet at this point, creating a source of power first used for the textile industry and later for silk production, both of

212

which enriched the city of Paterson for many years. Prosperity, however, had been marred more than once by labor unrest.

Sam glanced in that direction, but his thoughts seemed to be elsewhere. Mid looked for a place they could pull in and enjoy the picnic she had prepared: fresh peaches tucked neatly between ham sandwiches and pieces of Nana's famous layered chocolate cake. The basket's contents were covered by a light blanket Mid had knitted herself.

"I didn't make those professional connections at medical school. I'm not sure why. I guess I just studied and learned and assumed the right jobs would appear before me." He shrugged and shifted his feet in the bottom of the boat. "Well, and the job did appear at St. Anne's, but I'm not sure the particular path that's opening up is the one I want."

"Speaking of paths, see that little sandy spot there, with grass behind it? Shall we stop? I've made us a nice lunch."

"Ah, yes. I see." He lowered the oars and began to pull for the shore. "It's hard when you have to work . . . to work for the money. My family is eager for me to begin my practice. There are still some debts . . . Of course, anyone who has any kind of job today should feel lucky, but . . . "

Mid saw his mind wandering as the boat had been drifting earlier.

"When you're back at Archer in the fall," he went on, as the boat's hull scraped the sand. "I will be coming to Baltimore now and then. My aunt and uncle live nearby; that's one reason I went to school

213

there in the first place. Maybe you could introduce me to some of these doctor friends of yours. Who knows, perhaps they will need another researcher in the future."

Mid hoped that giving a boost to his career was not "the change" Frances Border prophesied for her. Nor was Sam to be the "traveler" thought to be "in danger"--well, unless he gave Mid a chance to push him into the river.

Chapter 30: Homecoming

Uncle Henry was standing on the front porch when Mid returned to Ridge Road early that evening. Assuming he had come to visit his sister-- and perhaps even work toward a reconciliation with Nana--she was pleased. However, when she got closer, the look on his face, even grimmer than when she'd visited him earlier in the week, made her stop short.

"What is it? Are you all right? Your symptoms are worse?"

"It's not me, Marian. It's your father . . . he's ill."

Mid started to push past him into the house, but he held her by one arm. "Wait a moment and let me explain. Your mother has taken something, a sedative, and is resting upstairs. Dr. Paterson was here earlier. Alice is with her."

"It's that's bad? Where is father? Oh, tell me what's happened?"

"He's at Union Memorial Hospital in Baltimore. He became unwell during a business meeting. At first, he thought he would just go back to his hotel and rest, but he collapsed at the elevator. And they had to call an ambulance."

"What . . . ? Oh, I must go immediately. I know Baltimore. And I can get help from . . . from my professors."

"Your brother John is already on the way. Curtis' business associates knew to contact him. We need you to stay here with Ethel. She . . . she didn't take this at all well."

Mid thought about Mother's plan to leave the house for an unspecified length of time, pursuing her writing in Brooklyn or somewhere. It probably seemed now almost like a betrayal of responsibility.

"Do the doctors know what . . . are they treating him?"

It began to sink in that this was quite serious. Even though she had felt surprise at first, her belief in the underlying order of things kept telling her this was a temporary situation, a difficult period they would get through. And then, in a few days or a week, her life would return to normal. The Lacy family would be whole as always.

Uncle Henry escorted her into the living room. They sat down beside each other on the sofa. "They think it might be Curtis' heart. At the hospital he spoke of chest pain. He's been working so hard, Ethel says; he may just be succumbing to exhaustion."

Mid didn't think he'd shown signs of strain at Camp Robin. She began to wonder about others. "Is Grandpa all right?"

"We haven't told him yet. Nana explained that he's become a bit confused from time to time, his memory playing tricks on him. You've probably noticed. So, right now, we can let him think Curtis is continuing with his business trip."

"Ella?"

"She will be here tomorrow, with the baby. You girls have to support your mother now. I believe your father will recover in time, but . . . but, well, God's will be done."

Uncle Henry's composure, despite his genuine concern for the family, must be connected, Mid thought, to the Catholic influence of his boarding house. Or perhaps to some sort of dark Presbyterian belief in preordination, as if our destinies had been laid out from the beginning of time, and all the family could do was endure with the hope of fulfillment in the next world. She couldn't accept God's will if He meant the loss of her father.

Since Ella was coming, though, she realized they were in crisis. With Ax struggling, how did her sister find money for travel, unless . . . unless Uncle Henry or Ethel offered to pay? But, again, if that were true, Mid foresaw the worst. She wondered if Henry was telling her all he knew.

When she arrived the next day, Ella was even more distraught than Mid. Of course, she'd been the dramatic sister all along. What struck Mid, though, was how . . . well, how disheveled she was. Her hair had tangles, her clothes seemed to have been thrown on at the last minute, there had been no effort to "do her face." Ella had always looked good, even when caught up in a whirlwind of activity. But the shock of the unexpected, or motherhood, or hard times had had their effect.

"Oh, Marian," she said when they were alone in their old room. "What are we going to do?"

"Do? Why, we have to stay here, take care of Mother, wait to hear from John." No other options had occurred to her. John had only telegraphed to say he was in Baltimore with Father.

"But . . . but we have to *do* something. Get Alice and Nana. We must have a meeting." Since it wouldn't do any harm and might provide an outlet for Ella's anxiety, Mid agreed.

Shortly the four women were gathered around the dining room table. Grandpa was in his room, where he usually went after lunch to read, doze, and visit his farm in memory. Having slept through the night and learning that John was with Curtis, Ethel had gone up to her study to read. She told the girls she wanted to be alone with Henry for a time when he returned. He had gone back to Waypoint House the evening before.

"Curtis is a young man," Nana asserted. She spoke softly, as they all would. "*Ach weh*, he just needs to rest. He works too hard. You girls know that."

"We should have seen it coming," Ella said tearfully. "Oh, I don't mean to blame any of you. I haven't been to visit, but the baby . . . " Little Pete was asleep in her arms.

Mid explained, "I was with him last weekend at the Lake, and he was fine. He went about all the little chores he meant to accomplish and never complained of tiring." When she thought back about it, though, Mid did wonder if he'd seemed out of breath a couple of times. Of course, she could be imagining that now, in retrospect exaggerating the effects of normal exertion. Still, she began to feel a slow panic growing inside her.

Alice added. "Ella, he walked to the station when he left home, as he always does." His office had his luggage taken to the train for him on business trips. "I saw him, and, you know how briskly he goes. There was no change. And he was eager to take this trip."

Mid realized that Alice, though years younger, was more under control than Ella. In fact, her even speech and deliberate movement resembled Uncle Henry's, as if she'd found an unexpected source of spiritual strength. Was the priest at Holy Trinity Episcopal, Father James, more of an influence on her than anyone had realized?

Nana brought her Old World perspective to the discussion. "Girls, we have to be strong now. My family has been tried, back home and in this country. Your mother and I . . . well, we had to survive hard times until Curtis came into our life. Grandfather was gone, and Henry . . . Henry was unable to marry. There were reasons, but . . . And, *Der Himmell sei Dank,* your father! He is a Lacy, descended from the first settlers of Nantucket. They built a nation, with God's help. So, will we in that spirit continue."

Mid wanted to know what Uncle Henry and Nana had said to each other the day before. She knew Ethel had called him to come to Ridge Road, but mother and son must have been together at some point in the last twenty-four hours. Was his star-crossed love long ago the reason for his estrangement from his family?

"Why didn't John give us a telephone number to call?" Ella wailed. "We're stuck here, away from what's happening. It's so frustrating to be . . . to be where, where nothing is going on, just life as usual, when you're needed somewhere else."

Mid had another of her visions: the faraway city, a hospital emergency, doctors and nurses--and medical technologists--called from sleep by an emergency. One young (but mature) woman helps the injured, though she wears a lab coat not a uniform. A building has collapsed, children are pulled from the rubble, and a handsome doctor calls, "We have to do a blood serum analysis. Is there anyone here who's trained? It's a life or death situation."

Alice said quietly, "Why don't we pray?"

"How can you all be so calm?" exclaimed Ella, jumping up from the table and pacing around the room.

Rather than feeling the steadiness her imagined self might demonstrate in Singapore or Johannesburg or wherever, the real Mid in Rutherford felt she was coming apart, beside herself with worry, confusion, self-doubt.

When, later that night, the call came from John, not even Uncle Henry was calm. The three sisters threw their arms around their mother and each other, unrestrainedly weeping. Still, it was Mid who had enough composure to hear someone open the front door and walk down the hall.

She stepped out to see her brother Bill. The broad smile on his boyish, tan face was clearly in expectation of a hero's welcome. It faded in front of her drawn face.

She went to him. "Father's dead, Bill. We've got to get ready for a funeral."

Volume Four: Out of Touch.
Chapter 31: Signals

"Did we lose our signal again," called Mid. "Or have they interrupted the broadcast?"

She was on the brick patio behind the kitchen, playing cribbage with Tony. In Macopin, the old set Mother had brought from Ridge Road couldn't always pull in their favorite radio stations. Right now, Mid wanted to tune in for "Freddy Partner's Musical Party."

"They're pausing for another statement by the President," Alice answered, cracking the screen door to look out. She was baking cookies. "More grim war news, I'm sure." Now a member of Holy Trinity Episcopal Church, she was especially concerned about the bombing of London and the destruction of Anglican landmarks.

Marian was enjoying the summer evening. But these days she couldn't shake a conviction that any peaceful moment might be interrupted by unsettling news from somewhere--the latest base Bill had traveled to, Diana's West Virginia, the last free countries of Europe.

"It's your deal, sweetheart," whispered Tony, handing her the cards. "If anything is happening, we'll hear soon enough."

He'd asked Mid before why she was so nervous these days. It was uncharacteristic of her, the Lacy always counted on for stability and control.

However, the biggest interruption of events she could have ever imagined, her father's death, had established a pattern: nothing could be counted on forever. The distant can impose on the close at hand, tragically.

Other losses had come after her father's death. As hopes for peace were diminishing around the globe at the end of the decade, it seemed as if the Lacy men were deliberately deserting their women. Less than a year after Curtis (it *was* his heart that gave out), Grandpa and Uncle Henry passed away, the latter, according to the doctor, a victim of old age. He'd not lived so many years, but they had been difficult ones. Nana's health went down quickly after finally revealing to Mid the rest of her son's sad history. She was buried in Brooklyn beside her husband.

Then, home from China for what seemed to the rest of the family a short time, Bill had enlisted in the Army Air Corps and was soon in Texas. When Hitler invaded Poland, he said, "This war will spread around the world. And I have friends in China. We have to help."

Even his mother's widowhood didn't sway him. "Mid will do better keeping the house than I ever would," he argued. "And she would hardly be volunteering to go off and fight in a war."

John and Axel believed the United States should stay out of this Old World conflict, though their own work in finance and telephone systems was becoming increasingly international. With America gearing up its industrial might to supply allied armies, their responsibilities meant Ethel and her two unmarried daughters were more and more on their own.

There was, of course, the boy next door. Tony Giordano, back from Spain and living at home. He wasn't "next door" any longer, though, the Ridge Road house having proven too much to handle for the women. Still, he was a regular visitor at their new home. They moved to a snug little cottage twenty-five miles from Rutherford, passing the Lacy family house on to Axel and Ella, who needed room for their growing family and were unable to buy on their own.

Out in Macopin, Mid felt isolated from the most important events of her lifetime: the spreading war in Europe, continuing economic strife at home, the progress of medical science--especially after her last years at Archer as a member of an exciting physiology laboratory program. The Fit Female Program, she had to admit, went on in the protected realm of a woman's school, not at a major center of scientific research. She felt the sporadic radio reception in this hilly area underscored her continuing tangential connection to larger currents of change.

Tony always brought the latest news, but she feared he was taking her warm welcome too much as a romantic signal only, not also as an eagerness to feel part of history. She was being courted by a man who had seen the world--twice. True, she liked Tony more than she ever had, but there was the obstacle of religion: would she have to convert to Catholicism?

After a longer recovery from being a prisoner of war than had been predicted, Tony began working as a trolley conductor, not only because his father had connections with the union, but also because the company was impressed with his military experience. His irregular hours limited trips to Macopin, but it was clear this was where he wanted to be.

Mid did travel by herself to Wayne on many weekends, filling in at St. Joseph's Hospital when men wanted to be home with their families. And that provided some sense of involvement with national affairs. But, as a substitute medical technologist, she felt she was still responding to needs defined by others, not setting a course for herself. And her work was often routine, without the new procedures and exciting ideas that Dr. Royal had brought to her.

"Mid," Tony asked while she was shuffling for her turn as dealer. "Do you realize there are going to be opportunities for medical personnel overseas, once we're drawn into this war?"

They'd had talks about what would happen in the future, he firmly convinced that America would not be able to stay on the sidelines and she still holding to her father's opinion that we had too much self-interest in staying neutral.

Mid heard the radio resolve from static. The President had apparently finished his chat, and now one of the Big Bands was serenading the nation.

"One of my professors, Dr. Royal, says we'll be able to assume important positions at home when the men go abroad. And I would hate to leave

225

Mother to worry about Alice by herself." Alice acted as if she were engaged to Father James Scott, but he'd not sought Mother's permission; so, according to Ethel's etiquette, Alice was still free.

"It's possible for husband and wife to serve together overseas: nurse and ambulance driver, or medical technologist and military personnel." This wasn't the first time he'd speculated about a future they might share. And she admitted that he had changed since that summer day before the Rutgers Astronomy camp, when he had knelt beside her in the garden and suggested they make a commitment to each other. She had changed as well, but whether the college graduate she was wanted to become the wife he desired was not easy to decide.

The old dream of herself in some distant place-- jungle or desert or frozen landscape--returned regularly. She saw herself called into action by the unexpected. There was always an accident, injuries, a need for calm and clarity. Trained and tried, she was the one who steps forward, if not as the man in charge, at least as a competent organizer.

"There's been a cave-in at the gold mine," she imagines a rattled senior nurse telling her, trying to keep a crowd of native families in South Africa from overhearing. They're alarmed that the lift is not bringing miners to the surface. "But help is on the way. We're just waiting for someone who can organize blood donors. We're going to . . . we may have to have transfusions."

The mine's manager rushes past, two assistants trailing. The natives run after him. Seeing them, the nurse says, "There's sure to be trouble."

Mid takes her by the arm and gives her a shake. "Tell them we're setting up a first aid station." She looks around. "Clear out one of those large tents--two tables, folding chairs--put them there!" She points. "Get signs with red crosses on them and call for volunteers. Go now!"

The nurse seems paralyzed. "But . . . but . . . "

"I'll take the responsibility. I'm not sure what we'll need, but if it looks like we know and that we're doing something, we can prevent confusion. But it has to be done *now*. I'll go get supplies, some lab equipment, bandages and splints. Do you hear?"

". . . pack my things and go." These words from the radio interrupted her reverie.

"Wait!" Mid said abruptly to Tony, stopping him in the middle of the deal with a raised hand. She cocked her head, hearing a beautiful light voice singing. It was oddly familiar.

"Back Water Blues that calls me to pack my things and go."

It was the very song Bart Stuart had sung years ago at Greenwood Lake, his evocative rendition floating across the water from their house to Camp Robin. She'd thought it a girl's voice. Then, spying on the family, she had moved her attention to the brother, Sydney.

"What is it?" Tony asked. "It's just music, not news."

She turned back to him, smiling. "I know. It just reminded me . . . "

He looked indulgently at her, his affection visible.

"Mmm, I can't move no more/ Mmm, I can't move no more / There ain't no place for a poor old girl to go."

The voice was so similar to the one she'd heard years ago, or to what she remembered hearing, that it brought back that sweet summer of her youth, a time made impossibly remote by the death of her father, the terrible approach of war, a confrontation with the social limits a girl could not overcome.

Then the announcer said, "We're pleased to welcome back to the microphone a talented young singer who will be a regular on our show for the next month, Bartholomew Stuart."

This, she thought, "Might be the very call for which I've been longing?"

Chapter 32: "The Smoke of Love"

Mid's best friend at St. Joseph's, Martha Hartman, was a native of Manhattan. The daughter of a prominent attorney, she often attended events in the city as a guest of one of her father's clients or as a companion to another member of her well-to-do family. She had a standing invitation to join the studio audience for "Freddy Partner's Musical Party" and, just this week, had offered Mid the chance to accompany her.

She had already taken Mid on two memorable excursions: the "Britain at War" exhibit at the Museum of Modern Art and "Watch on the Rhine." She was moved by Lillian Hellman's Broadway drama of a German-born engineer, who'd fled his home country and then tried to help the friend who rescued him from the Gestapo. If she went with Martha to see Freddy Partner, would she also see Bart Stuart? Could that possibly lead to another meeting with Sydney?

"It's so much fun to go backstage and meet the performers," Martha had told her. "You'd think the stars would be so stand-offish, they wouldn't even bother to talk. But they're always so polite and so nice. Why Freddy himself shook my hand!"

Martha was a floor nurse at St. Joseph's, who liked to take her breaks with Mid. She could join her friend for coffee in the lab and sometimes arranged to meet her for lunch.

"I have to make sure my sister is home with Mother," Mid explained. "Alice is helping with a . . . with a school for children. And her hours vary from week to week."

She was reluctant to explain that this was a government program, designed to allow family members to work or to look for jobs in the continuing hard times. The Lacy family generally felt people in need could just try harder and pull themselves up from poverty, but Alice had different views. Once again, Father James was suspected of introducing these dangerous ideas.

Martha and Mid were sitting on a bench outside the hospital this afternoon. The weather lingered in a rich autumn, as if winter were being magically kept at bay. Mid was nervous about how Mother would react to longer nights and darkened days. Since Curtis' death, she had turned away from many friends; and then they moved away to the quieter, country home.

"She's romantically involved, isn't she?" Martha asked. "Your sister."

"Well, she has a young man, the priest at the Episcopal church in Rutherford. But there's nothing formal. He doesn't make very much money, and Mother hopes she'll finish her studies at the State Teachers' College before they even think of marrying."

"Well, I'll give you advance notice for the show. Maybe my brother can escort us."

Mid thought it would be unwise for Alice to marry so young, as Ella had. Well, too, if Alice left home, Mid's old prediction of her becoming the maiden aunt who stays home to take care of parents might be realized. If Mother could just settle into the Macopin community more, Mid could begin to look for a position that was more rewarding--financially and professionally.

At home Mid was also frustrated at being drawn into increasingly frequent discussions of religion. Alice had taken her confirmation classes at Holy Trinity very seriously, and Ethel was reading her Bible regularly. One Lacy woman was drawn toward a high liturgical church with strong traditions, while the other wanted unfettered connection with God through His Word. Mid--much more a scientist than a believer--had become the sounding board for both sides.

As far as Mid could tell, Mother was not writing poetry, at least not in the way she had hoped before Curtis died. She would look up from her desk with her characteristic, dreamy expression, but the page open in her lap was scripture, not Tennyson or Browning.

One day, though, Mid did see her Mother's journal open on her desk. Feeling a bit of a spy, she still read the short, handwritten poem she saw there. It was called "Azalea," but Mid was sure it referred to Father.

> *Beloved,*
>
> *Deep in the shadowed woods*
> *I saw your eyes and your hands -*
> *But when I had cleared from my eyes*

231

The smoke of love,

You were gone.

Perhaps new compositions were being added, memorable products of grief.

Any chance Mid had to slip away from home for an outing, then, was welcome, even if it might come without complications. And Martha's brother, who might end up going with them to Freddy Partner's Party, was very much a complication.

Dr. Roger Hartman was Mid's boss at St. Joseph's, the laboratory's director. And he sometimes lingered at her station longer than official business required. He might ask about her Rutherford growing up, the Fit Female research, her internships at St. Anne's. While Mid enjoyed his company, she also knew he was married. And his behavior bordered on flirtation.

According to what she'd learned from Martha, his was an unusual union. He lived in Passaic, while Mrs. Hartman had her own apartment in Manhattan. Samantha Hart (her stage name) was a mostly unemployed actress, but claimed she needed to be close to her agent and producers if she was going to reach the stardom she felt was her destiny. Mid couldn't help wonder how she filled all her free hours without a regular job--and no children.

Still, Mid had to admit that Dr. Hartman was attractive and his attentions flattering. A large man with movie star looks, he was a skilled conversationalist. A lot of the girls sighed when he deigned to speak with them, though his comments were sometimes, Mid thought, a bit risqué.

"There you are, Marian," he observed when he came into the lab one morning. "There you are, elevated like a goddess to be worshipped. Should I go down on my knees?"

In order to measure liquids that would be poured into beakers, Mid was perched on her high stool. His gaze, though, was not directed where a crown might be but at the slit in the front of her lab coat opening just above her knees. Though she would never be tall, Mid knew she had good legs. And she knew that good legs mattered.

"By no means! I'm just making sure I have the right amounts of medium. They made these lab counters for men, and we ladies sometimes have to perch to do our work."

There was not really a word for "sexy" in those days, though it lay behind many of the regular phrases used to describe attractive women: "she has a great figure"; "what a Sheba!"; "a regular glamour girl." To peel back the surface of any of them led to the term "lust," and no respectable man thought of himself as drawn by that force.

"Still, I see you up on a pedestal, wearing that clean white coat, your hair done up nicely, the bloom of youth on your cheeks."

"I'm a working woman, Dr. Hartman, not a princess. No supreme beings are given weekend shifts at a Catholic hospital."

She unhooked one heel from the stool's rung and lowered it to the floor, raising herself as if she needed a different vantage point. She felt his gaze descend to her calf and turned her head to see if she could catch him.

He looked up. "We American men admire our women, from the girl next door to our stars on the silver screen. They're all beautiful, active, enjoying the good things of life." His voice went measurably softer. "Though, you, Mid . . . you may be special . . . a delicious treat to some lucky man, a tasty morsel."

This kind of talk was new to Mid, whose male admirers had praised her looks in conventional phrases, but not hinted that they were drawn to her physically.

"Oh, I'm playing the field, Dr. Hartman. My father said there are many fish in the sea." She laughed. "Of course, he was really talking to my brothers."

She refused even to count Sydney as a potential fish in the sea. After all, it was Alice he'd stolen a kiss from years ago, and Mid had simply been escorted by him to a play. She still received occasional correspondence from him, but at their last meeting, on the shore of Greenwood Lake, he had kept his distance, perhaps in order to romance another woman.

"There are of all types of creatures in the sea, Miss Lacy--including octopuses who would hold you and sharks that would eat you up."

Mid looked toward the hall, hoping--or worrying--that someone would come in and break up their little tête-à-tête. "It's a lucky thing, then, I'm a good swimmer."

"Hmm, a regular Gloria Marie Callen, I'm sure. I'd

love to watch you in the water." His look suggested he was imagining her in a swimsuit.

"Is Mrs. Hartman a good athlete? Perhaps you two are regular sports partners?"

"Well, we . . . we used to be, but now I'm so busy with work, and she has her career." It almost seemed that he was going to reach out touch her on the arm . . . or somewhere else. "Anyway, I think *you're* a real sweetheart."

Chapter 33: Communicating with Spirits

Many nights at their little house in Macopin Mid lay awake thinking about the woman she had become compared to the poetic image of her Dr. Paterson had created. She was far less ethereal than that angel in verse, much more a body that yearned for contact with others.

When the wind drifted through the window of her bedroom, with the scent of apples ripening in the field behind their house, she felt a powerful urge to hold in her hands materials that connected her to others. This house itself was a microcosm of what she desired.

The front door opened into a large central room with a cathedral ceiling and a slim balcony along the back wall. Three small bedrooms opened onto the balcony, one at the top of the open stairway on the left wall and two along the back. Behind the great room on the first floor were a dining room and kitchen; on the right wall stood a large stone fireplace and chimney. At the back under the stairway on the left, a door opened to another room and the bath. The great room drew everything together; the walls joined rather than separated; it seemed as if you could reach out and touch anyone else in the house.

When the nine members of her childhood family gathered at meal times in their three-story Ridge Road house, Mid had felt crowded by the fierce spirit of Lacy New England individualism. Perhaps because there were only three in Macopin--and those all women--there Mid felt a stronger sense of connection. And she wished to extend it into other areas.

The experience of sisterhood at Archer, especially strong in the Fit Female Program, had tapped a desire in her to be part of a community in motion-- that is, to participate in the making of a communal history. Perhaps that's why her feelings for Tony had changed since their high school days. Despite the strain of his first service in Spain, he had gone back a second time, believing that conflict a sign of potential larger wars to come. He would not take himself out of the world's destiny, even though, according to some, he had earned that right.

Mid recalled her history professor, Dr. Fahr, who loved the idea of the America frontier. He'd taught her that we're a people who turn their backs on the past, convinced we deserve a fresh start. The future must offer us a clean slate somewhere--the New World for the first European settlers, the prairie and beyond to the next generation traveling in wagon trains, a mythical, fruit filled California even now for the Okies fleeing the Dust Bowl along Route 66.

But wasn't the world going to run out of space to let us begin again and again and again? If so, we had to take a stand where we are and at this time. Her mentors at Archer were making their commitment through a belief that powerful women were necessary to the nation's future. They were creating their own examples of physical strength like Diana and were training others like Mid to use their intellectual force in new fields. Mid wanted to identify an existing place where she could act, not escape to some open field to claim as her own.

The model for active woman represented by her mother and her older sister was wife and mother. They were involved in church and civic affairs, but their primary reason to be on the planet seemed to be to produce and nurture other people who would live on the planet. They didn't have much of a hand in determining what that life would be.

She heard regularly from Diana Tracy, whose uncle had rescued her family and allowed her to finish Archer. She was back in West Virginia teaching women how to make gardens more productive, family meals more nutritious, children better educated at home. She traveled by horse to remote farms and met stiff resistance from a people who resented anyone, even a native, telling them how to farm, cook, and sew. But Diana embraced the challenge, her physical abilities matched by the confidence that had come with her education. She was an ambassador of the future to her home region; and women especially responded to her unwavering conviction that things could be made better

"I am jealous of you," Mid wrote her friend. "I mainly manage the house and only get to be in the lab a couple of days a week. And the work I do is testing, not exploring. You, on the other hand, are changing lives, using your abilities in a good cause."

"In all my journeys," Diana wrote back, "I am sustained by God, by my friends, and by one man.

You are still my coach, Marian, and your letters always cheer me."

Mid was reluctant to ask directly about this "one man," a possible lover. Still, she tried to create opportunities for Diana to say more.

"I have one old friend," she wrote back, " a neighbor from Rutherford, who calls on us. He and I grew up together, so we share a past. Is the man you mention someone new in your life?

But Diana was evasive in her responses, and Mid couldn't learn much about this mystery suitor. She concluded that the two saw each other infrequently but continued their relationship by mail. Something Diana wrote once suggested he might be in Pennsylvania, but what he did, who his family were, how seriously he took the relationship was unclear.

In bed this particular night, Mid speculated about Diana's long-distance romance and then wondered what to do about the strange letter from afar she'd received earlier that day. It had been addressed to a "Miss Lacy" on Ridge Road, Rutherford, but forwarded to Macopin. Mid thought it might have been addressed to Alice. The letter, she soon realized, was for her, though it might have been delivered from the moon as been posted--as it had been--in Salinas, Kansas.

"Dear Miss Lacy," it began. "You won't know who this is from, unless, as I fervently hope, you are the girl I met six or seven years ago near Memorial Plaza in St. Louis. Even if you were that girl, you might not remember the boy who spoke to you in a bookstore nearby. You were examining a copy of *Harper's*

239

Magazine that included a story about Mark Twain; and I told you the history of his 'Platonic Sweetheart.'"

Fortunately, Mid was alone in her room, already lying on her bed, when she read this. Otherwise, she was sure, she would have fallen to the floor.

Her winter journey to the middle of the country had surfaced from memory a number of times when she was at Archer and afterwards. It sometimes worried her that the encounter with a boy who wanted to be the next Einstein might turn out to have occurred during the last time she ever left her native state. But the recollection of this boy's infectious enthusiasm also generated an odd warmth. She had turned down, if reluctantly, his offer to take her to site of the 1904 World's Fair; and she concluded later that saying no might have been the loss of a special destiny. How would she react should a similar opportunity appear before her now?

"If you are that 'Miss Lacy,'" she read. "Please don't throw this away without listening to the rest of my story. First, I'll tell you how I decided you might be my visitor to Missouri."

"The purse you had on your arm that day had a post card with the name 'Lacy' written on it. You hugged the bag to you when I first spoke. That made me look, and I read the name." Mid had, in fact, bought several picture post cards that day and addressed them in the bookstore to keep them from becoming mixed up. One was to Glenna, another to Mother and those at home, one to Ella, a final card for John in Boston.

"You told me you were from Rutherford, so, I had clues that led me to this address and the hope that you live here."

Mid realized that the boy--well, by now surely a man--was leaving out some steps in the process of finding her. A name and a town would not be enough, she reasoned, to lead to a specific address, unless he had a telephone book or some other listing of local residents. How he'd proceeded, though, was less important at this moment than why.

"Now I approach the hardest part of my search for a girl I spoke with for less than half an hour more than half a decade ago. It's quite possible--if, again, you are the Lacy I hope you are--that this letter and my wish are already in the waste basket. I hope that they are not."

My goodness, thought Mid: is he going to ask me to marry him! She recalled Tony's proposal by mail from the summer astronomy institute several years before her trip to St. Louis. Were her most interested lovers the farthest away!

The Missouri letter continued. "You might say that I was a medium that day, contacting Mark Twain from wherever in the great beyond his ghost roams in order to reach out to you. And he had his own medium, conjuring up a Platonic Sweetheart from his dreams. I hope this letter draws you out of the ether so that you can become . . . my 66 Sweetheart. I'll explain what that means in a second letter, but I'm giving you time first to remember me."

The letter was signed, "A Scientist."

Mid imagined the spirit of this quixotic dreamer sliding in her bedroom window with the scent of apples, flowing over the bed, around the corner past Mother's room, down into the center of the house below, where it settled before the hearth as if it would one day reside there, a permanent member of the family.

Chapter 34: Prospects

"Mid," her mother said after breakfast the next morning. "Tony has been calling on you a lot these past few months." Ethel had been working the *Times* crossword and was looking at her daughter over the folded paper. Alice had already taken an early bus to her school in Wayne.

"He's good company, Mother. I like to hear what he thinks about the war . . . and other things."

"Yes, he is very caught up in current events--I guess, because of family in his home country. Maria is worried about her nephews, who have been forced to enlist in Mussolini's army. She says they have no choice. And everyone is afraid to try to leave the country."

"Where would they go? It's dangerous even to travel by sea these days."

"Yes. Well, anyway . . . that's not really what I wanted to talk about. I was thinking of you and Tony. You're seeing so much of each other, I just wandered if you've considered what . . . what marriage means?"

Oh, dear, Mid thought to herself. Is this going to be a lecture about the birds and the bees? But it could also be about faith. Tony had told her he knew several successful mixed couples, though in each case the children were receiving a Catholic education.

"Mother, he hasn't proposed. And if he did, I'm not sure what my answer would be. He doesn't know what his future holds. It seems to me we're all in a period of transition, waiting for the outcome of so many events at home and away. We're between the end of one period and the beginning of something new we don't fully understand."

She thought of herself as in between stages personally as well. Since her father's death and her graduation from Archer, she'd been content to focus on family, especially her mother. John, of course, had handled all the legal and financial matters involving the estate, while she sustained the domestic routine and then supervised the move into the country. There hadn't been time to explore in what ways she might move on herself.

"Perhaps there are other young men you're interested in? You don't say much about who you see at St. Joseph's, but you and your friend have been into the city several times."

"Martha Hartman, the nurse, yes. In fact, she's invited me to go with her to Freddy Partner's Music Party this weekend, but there are no men involved." Mid decided this white lie was forgivable. After all, it wasn't definite that Martha's brother would be going with them. "And," she admitted, "all the . . . interesting . . . men at St. Joseph's are already taken."

"I see." There was a pause. Mid took up her knitting again while Mother returned to the crossword. But apparently she wasn't done. "I was thinking . . . you know how hard Ella works with her boys, Axel so busy at work. Ruth, too, has learned that being a wife is time consuming."

"There are married women who keep working before they have children, though," said Mid. "And some women, nurses like Martha, can take their jobs back once their children are older and in school. Mother, are you thinking I need to find a husband who can provide for me?"

She said it almost jokingly, not thinking there could be any strain on Mother's resources. John had assured them that Father, an insurance man all his adult life, had made generous financial provisions for Ethel and her children in the event of his own death.

"I wasn't thinking about that at all. It was more a feeling that you actually enjoy your hospital work. You certainly did take to the research program at Archer. I know it's hard right now to find a good job, especially for a woman, but once married . . . it becomes even harder."

Oh, Mid thought. Is she thinking I might not need to marry at all? And does she believe I should pursue the career Father thought was only to fill in the gap between school and motherhood?

She remembered Mother's plan to take a sabbatical from her role at Ridge Road and devote herself to writing poetry. Was she thinking that-- when she married at a young age--she had lost out on the chance to be an author, like Elizabeth Barrett Browning or Edna St. Vincent Millay? And did she now hope at least one of her daughters could pursue a similar dream?

Mid said, "I have been wondering, now that you mention it, if, after a while, I might need to expand my search for the right laboratory to apply to. There may be more opportunities in . . . in different areas." She was reluctant to say how far such a search could take her from Macopin.

"I think," Mother concluded, "you might write to one of your professors, that Dr. Royal you've told me about. See what she recommends. I'm sure she has professional associations outside of Maryland, perhaps up our way."

"I . . . I can do that. I would want to be sure Alice was still here with you. I couldn't bear to think of you all alone out here in the country."

"Oh, you don't need to worry about me. I've been meeting with some new friends, who feel the same way I do about the Bible. We're considering starting our own church. Mr. Smithson--you've met him--has offered his house for meetings, now that all his children are grown. It would have a lot in common with the church Father liked so much. I will be very busy."

Mid would later look back on this conversation as pivotal in both their lives. It wouldn't turn out that Ethel threw herself into the project of founding what would become Calvary Bible Chapel for another year. Nor did Mid move away from Macopin immediately, as national and international events closed in on America--even on women who never imagined they would be directly involved in the business of war.

However, the realization that her mother understood a young woman's aspirations and was encouraging her to seek fulfillment outside of marriage was important to Mid. If two offers of marriage had not come to her this year, she might have pursued a life much more like her female mentors at Archer. Nonetheless, mother and daughter were at separate crossroads in their lives that fall. And both were soon on courses whose ends they could not foresee at that moment.

At the same time, Mid's most ardent suitor, Tony Giordano, was preparing for a change as well. Ever since Mussolini met with Hitler at Rastenberg, his concern for his home country had been growing. And, though he came to see Mid as frequently as ever, she realized he was considering volunteering to serve wherever he could in support of the anti-Fascist cause.

The same week in which Mother asked about their relationship, Tony talked with Mid about the situation in Europe. Again, they were playing cribbage, but, as winter had arrived, it was on the sofa by the stone fireplace. Mother and Alice were upstairs writing letters or reading.

"What I can't understand," Tony began, "is how so many people think we can sit this one out."

The Lacy family cribbage board had three scoring tracks, though three-way games were rare. For some reason, perhaps an odd sense of propriety, Mid (red) and Tony (blue) used the outside scoring lanes and kept the center (white) lane open between their pieces.

"I guess our parents' generation remembers the Great War. Even though we got into it late, there were terrible losses."

"I know. My family's village lost many young men, almost a generation. But that was a war between kings; this is a war to preserve freedom against dictatorship. Hitler is deep into Russia, and I don't see how England can hold out without our support."

"If we are drawn in, do you know what you'll do?" She held her hand on her red scoring peg and looked intently at Tony.

He glanced up at the balcony. Mid had told him how no room in this house was cut off from the great one, especially when, as was the case tonight, doors were left open.

"All I can say right now is that I can't stand idly by when so much is at stake."

"So much at stake," thought Mid.

She remembered stories her father had told her about the first Lacys in this country: Thomas, the Quaker, who pulled up stakes in England to build a new society overseas; Nantucket shopkeeper John Lacy's son Rowland who founded the famous department store chain. They had forged their own destinies and created structures that continued their legacies. Shouldn't she determine the place where she could stand and dedicate herself to a cause? And what cause could be greater than the survival of the way of life built by her ancestors?

If Tony asked her, Mid concluded, she could become his wife, a support at home if he went away to war; but she might also work on the home front, or even go overseas as Dr. Royal had, helping the wounded and contributing to the advance of medical knowledge.

Her father, after all, came from his upstate farm to enter into the hustle and bustle of the busiest city in the world. Mother, even as she raised five children and cared for her hard working husband, wrote poetry that enlightened others. Mid, decided that, as their child, when the opportunity came, rather than withdraw from history she would enter into it with all her heart.

Chapter 35: Sights and Sounds

The radio studio impressed Mid, not only because there was so much equipment--microphones hanging from the ceiling, screens to block off sections of the stage, stands to hold scripts with headphones draped over the back--but also because she realized her mind had, from a distance, created a distorted picture of the scene.

"It must be the signal way out in Macopin," she told Martha. "The reception is undependable, coming in and going out; so I've gotten these fuzzy images in my head. This looks like it's under construction, with wires and supports that need to be installed somewhere."

She had imagined a traditional, formal concert hall, with rows of seats rising up from the stage and boxes on the sides. The floor here was flat, and there were only about two dozen plain metal folding chairs set up along the back wall for guests. The show's real audience took up no space, of course, being spread out in living rooms across the country.

Staff members were positioned around the room, most of them standing with clipboards or pieces of equipment. They wore informal work clothes rather than usher uniforms. Unlike at a traditional performance, it didn't matter if their bodies blocked the view of spectators. The goal of the operation was the gathering and transmission of something immaterial--sound.

If the hall was not magnificent, however, there were many aspects of the event that appealed to Mid, especially her closeness to the band. She could make out features of the performers as they were taking their places and setting up instruments.

She thought back to the time she had seen *Lost Horizons* with Sydney at the Hippodrome. While the actors portraying Mallison, Conway, and Lo-tsen had appeared right below her, the exotic characters they represented belonged, not just on the other side of the globe, but in another dimension entirely. These musicians were close to her; but, for people at home hundreds of miles away in every direction, they would seem to exist in the air, phantasms of a different realm.

She noticed a microphone on a stand to one side and at the front of the stage. It was positioned low, and someone in a wheelchair would be able to use it. Martha had given her a program, and Bartholomew Stuart's name was on it.

She tried to scan the other guests to see if Sydney was among them, but Roger, leaning close, distracted her with an almost steady stream of observation. Martha, on the other side, occasionally tried to bring the conversation back to more conventional topics.

"Freddy stays in his dressing room until the last minute. He says it's because he wants to save all his strength for the broadcast, but I think he's hiding in there with one of those very attractive make-up girls."

"They're all so professional," Martha explained. "The musicians, the sound crew, the directors. Everyone is dedicated to providing the best entertainment to the nation."

Mid wondered if Roger's wife, when she performed, was a dedicated professional or hid in the dressing room with a stage hand. He'd said she sometimes appeared on stage in other cities along the East Coast. Did she travel without her husband?

"This show is a vehicle to launch popular tunes and build a record-buying public," observed Roger. "Freddy always makes sure the female vocalists know he can give them a hand . . . in their careers, I mean."

"The singer today is a man," said Martha. "He's very talented."

Mid wondered if Roger was offering her a hand to advance her position at St. Joseph's . . . or a hand that would pull her into trouble.

One of the staff stepped to center stage and called for quiet: the show was about to begin. The musicians broke into the show's theme song, and Freddy Partner strode out as a microphone on a cable was lowered to him.

From some place off stage, an announcer, with a voice bigger and deeper than any Mid had heard, boomed out the familiar introduction: "Welllll--*come*, Partner *part*-ners. It's music time with your favorite band leader, Freddy Partner, and his special guest, on loan from Pittsburgh, Pennsylvania, the Oooo of Smooth, Bar-tho-looo-mew Stuart."

The music swelled, and Mid saw Bart roll out in his chair, gripping the rails on the outside of the wheels. (She'd speculated that Sydney might push him.) Locking the wheels, he stood slowly, using braces attached to his forearms. When he began to sing, Mid felt she'd heard this voice all her life, but that there was no chance the owner would know her among his listeners.

He was performing a current Hammerstein hit song: "*Paris is everybody's mistress, / Every man has his own secret memories of Paris.*" Since it was more than a year after the fall of the French city, there was poignancy in the lyrics. "*Her heart was warm and gay, / I heard laughter of her heart in every street cafe.*"

But Mid thought also about the last time she had been truly happy herself. Was it as long ago as when she went boating on the Passaic, believing that romance was the goal of Dr. Sam Bridges? Arriving back home, she had learned that her father had been struck down. And that single moment colored all her months since then. Even her college graduation, joyous in many ways, was marked by the absence of the most important man in her life.

Would Tony bring joy to her heart? When she had seen him at Archer, he was like the "*Lonely men with lonely eyes*" in the song Bart was singing. In the intervening years--a soldier again, a prisoner of war, finally a kind of prodigal son returned to the fold-- had he been "*seeking her in vain*"? Mid looked at Bart, but thought of Tony: "*The last time I saw Paris, her trees were dressed for spring, / And lovers walked beneath those trees and birds found songs to sing.*"

She was carried away by this first song and by the rest of the show. Bart sang three more times. Waiting, he studied the music on the stand before him and at times scanned the hall. Mid once saw his eyes pause on her, but there was no sign of recognition. At the intermission, however, a staff member brought her a folded note: "Please come to room 413 after the show."

Their meeting was brief, and, later, she forgot most of the standard pleasantries exchanged in such situations. But several comments remained with her a long time.

She found him chatting with other musicians. But he came to her and spoke easily, asking first about her mother.

"It's hard for her," Mid said, "but I think she's adjusted well . . . given the circumstances."

"I remember that picnic long ago at Greenwood Lake. You were kind to talk to me then. Some people find it awkward to talk to a man in wheelchair. And I was very sensitive then. You see that I can stand with braces now."

"That's wonderful! And you're certainly famous. Appearing in New York City, and I've heard you on the radio other times."

"Yes, it's been . . . remarkable. Father's connections helped give me a start, but I still have to perform. It's been a long road, with a few detours to many back country places."

"And your family, do they travel with you? Or is everyone back in Providence? Well, I guess they could be in any of your homes."

He laughed. "Oh, they're all over the place! Syd comes with me sometimes, but I also have an attendant who helps with travel. My base is Pittsburgh, as you heard. I have fans in that area. We travel throughout Pennsylvania, Ohio, West Virginia, little places like Youngstown, Elkins, Altoona. Our concerts in these places have generated a faithful radio audience. We have a special appeal, it seems, to people who are having a hard time of it."

"Music can be inspiring." Mid herself often felt swept away by the music she heard on the radio. "You play in your hometown as well? Do you want to move back there eventually?"

"I don't think so. At least not right now. I have made . . . some special friends where I am. I'm not ready to be away from them."

Mid paused, thinking about how she was away from so many people who mattered to her: her college friends, her brother Bill. Hasbrouck Heights, where Ella was--and even Rutherford--were removed from her daily life.

One of the staff, holding a clipboard, came into the room and gestured to Bart. Mid said, "I'd better be going. It's looks like you're wanted . . . out there. But I do have one question: how did you spot me out there? It was almost as if you knew I would be here this afternoon."

"Oh, I did know. We have mutual friends, Marian, you and I. And we should stay in touch--write me when you can." He handed her a card with a Pittsburgh address. Then he wheeled himself off as the staff member read instructions from his clipboard.

The mutual friends must include individuals in Martha's and Roger's circle, Mid concluded. Later, however, when she was leaving the building, she saw Sydney Stuart assisting someone--who looked like the same elegant woman she'd seen years ago at the Hippodrome--into a taxi. Were there other connections she did not see?

Chapter 36: Ghosts

"We have a letter from Bill," Mother said excitedly. "He's coming home!"

Mid had just gotten back from her excursion to the Freddy Partner show and was puzzling over what she had heard and seen at the radio studio.

"Home to stay?"

"That's what he writes. Here." She handed Mid the letter and went back into the kitchen, where she had been preparing a late supper. "Oh, and Alice is at Ella's. She had a late church service, and Father James drove her. She'll just go to her school from there in the morning."

This was an odd development. Ethel did not like Alice to stay away overnight with the priest as her escort. And it seemed even stranger with this news from Texas to share.

Mid learned that Bill had been assigned to the Fort Dix Airport. It was expanding its capacity for traffic in anticipation of possible war, but what this meant to Mid was that her younger brother would be close to home for the first time in some years.

"This is such good news," she told Mother, sitting on the stool in the little telephone nook between the kitchen and the dining room. "We can all be together again."

It seemed more and more likely that Ella and Axel would stay in Rutherford, John and Ruth in Hasbrouck Heights (they'd bought a house there),

Mother with her daughters in Macopin; so this would be better than at any point since Father's death. She did worry that Alice would marry Father James and move away, and her absence for this night increased that concern. But, even if it happened, Alice would likely stay in the area.

"I've never been comfortable with Bill being gone," Mother said, turning down the stove so the soup could continue to simmer. "It was bad enough when he was a missionary, and at such a young age; but a soldier! . . . well, anything can happen."

"Let's just pray that war never comes," Mid said, thinking not only about her brother, but also about Tony. She had to admit she had come to appreciate his long-term courtship. The other men who'd appeared in the role of possible suitor waxed and waned in their interest depending on how she complimented their dreams. She felt Tony's dreams had her at the center.

"Yes, nothing good ever comes from war." Mother had her distant look for a moment; then said, "Mid, would you look on my writing desk? My journal is on top." The little desk she'd had on the Ridge Road second floor landing fit nicely here in a corner beside a window, looking out toward the apple orchard behind the house. The journal was right at the center.

"Do you want me to bring it to you?"

"No, that's fine. Open to the last page that has writing on it. You'll see."

Mid brought it back with her to the kitchen stool, opened it, and read the short poem there, "Dead Tree."

Stark and

By no breeze bent,

Its hanging shreds of bark

Reveal the whitened nakedness

Of Death.

Mid exclaimed, "Mother! This is . . . well, it's sad. Did you write this recently?"

"No, I wrote it a long time ago, when you were just starting school."

"Why did you want me to see it now?

"Did Father ever tell you about his best friend, who died in the war?"

Mid hesitated. "I don't think so." She did recall Father's intensity when they were together at Greenwood Lake. He'd instructed her never to link her destiny to a soldier's. Perhaps his friend's death was the cause of that conviction.

"This poem is about him. Your father had told me what happened, and this was my attempt to help him come to terms with loss."

"I guess I don't understand," said Mid, reading the poem to herself again.

"It's bleak, I know; but what happened to Johnny was just as stark. Sometimes, I told Father, there can be no looking away. Although recently . . . I'm not so sure myself . . . "

"Father did tell me once that . . . that caring for a soldier is unwise."

"Johnny became a soldier. He was 'the most loyal friend a boy could ever have,' your father claimed. But the quality that made him loved as a boy killed him as a man."

Mother was ladling soup into two bowls and handing them to Mid, who asked, "They grew up together?"

"On neighboring farms. The played together, worked together, went to school together. They even came to New York on the same train to make their fortunes." She handed Mid a basket with bread warmed in the oven. "Then war came. Both men read the stories and saw the posters, which popped up everywhere, showing the evil 'Hun.' They were told that we had to fight to 'make the world safe for democracy.'"

Mother came to her place, and Mid asked, "Wasn't it also 'the war to end all wars'?"

"Yes, so they said. All those slogans had an effect. That's one reason I showed you the poem. I'll explain that in a minute. But first, please bless the food, and we can eat while we talk." Then she added, clearly as an afterthought, "Oh, and I do want to hear about the radio show." Both bowed their heads, and Mid gave the traditional, simple Lacy blessing: "*For what we are about to receive, oh Lord, make us truly grateful.*"

Mother had been so intense, first about Bill, then in telling Johnny's story, that Mid had forgotten for the moment her remarkable afternoon experience. The fact of Alice's approved absence was also moved to the back of her mind as Mother continued.

"There was one poster that really seemed to affect Johnny. On it there was a window that divided all young men: outside were soldiers marching in uniform; inside a comfortable, well-dressed man-about-town. The poster asked, 'On which side of the window are you?'"

"So a man could only be in one group or the other, no middle ground."

"Yes. Father, who came from a long line of Quakers--all the way back to Nantucket, really--did not believe in war. Still, he loved this country and, I think, would have defended it if we had been attacked directly. So he was not quite a pacifist, but neither was he convinced that Germany was the destroyer of all civilization."

"And Johnny was?"

"More than Father, certainly. What he couldn't get away from was that poster's lady-or-the-tiger dilemma. He didn't understand that there may be more than two choices."

Mid realized she'd been thinking in a similar fashion: there were men like Tony and her brother Bill, who felt compelled to take action, as opposed to others, Roger and Sydney, who seemed to float above the fray, unconcerned about the larger social welfare.

Mother went on. "There are some things, though, we can't disguise. That's why I showed you my poem. It doesn't lie. 'Dead tree' says death takes away all color, all protection. Your loved ones can preserve a reduced image of you in their hearts, but you no longer move in the wind and the memories

261

that trail off you are themselves without life. Language needs to be truthful, not twist reality into pretty images. And then we must accept what's there."

Mid wondered if Mother had truly accepted Father's death. Whether or not that was the case, Mid felt she was revealing thoughts she'd hidden throughout her life, just as she'd kept Dr. Paterson's poem about the angel child tucked among her papers. These powerful ideas were at play in the books Mother read, in her own poetry, and in the faraway look so often seen on her face.

Mid had also read at Archer some of the contemporary writers--Hemingway, especially--who rejected flowery prose for more direct, honest speech. She had to admit that the tone of those almost brutal, short sentences had an effect; they created a mood appropriate to the serious time in which they all lived. But she also suspected he was leaving out options, that there were more responses to events than what she found in his unyielding prose.

"So, what happened? Did Johnny enlist? Was he . . . killed?"

"Not exactly, or not immediately. He was blinded and lost the use of his limbs from horrible burns. They kept him in France for a year, and then shipped him back to a hospital in Washington, D.C. Your father traveled there to visit him . . . what was left of him."

"How awful!"

"Johnny begged him . . . to take his life, but Father couldn't do it. A few months later, he died anyway. But Curtis never got over it. And said he'd never support war for any reason."

Chapter 37: Dream Girl

Despite the terrible experience Father endured, and the lesson from it that Mother passed on to her, Mid still hoped Tony would ask for her hand. One of the reasons was that she found the idea of being someone's 66 Sweetheart almost frivolous in contrast. Before many months, however, events would change her mind about the nature of this opposition.

Because the first letter from Missouri had not called for a response, Mid had simply waited for a second. It came not long after the news that her brother was returning from Texas. "A Scientist" explained that, because his first letter hadn't come right back to him, he concluded that it had found her. And then he picked up where he'd left off.

"I am a student at Kansas Wesleyan College, and, each year, the college sponsors a song-writing contest, with the winner receiving a $100.00 prize to cover expenses at the school. Because times are so hard in our part of the country, I need every penny I can earn to finish my education. I am studying science and math and want to solve problems that have puzzled men over the centuries."

This much seemed admirable, if rather boastful. How Mid--or a 66 Sweetheart--was involved in the project, however, was unclear. She also found it odd that this man studied science, but was competing in another area. Was he a Renaissance man, skilled in many fields?

"Not only must each entry include music and lyrics, but we are supposed to write a brief account of the song's composition and then construct the artwork for an appropriate record cover. Believe it or not, my song was inspired by you."

Mid wondered how old this man was. Unless he had worked before going to college, he was probably at least four or five years younger than she, depending on what year he was in right now. The boldness of his letter, combined with a boyish assumption that he was pursuing a reasonable course, suggested he was still very young or, unfortunately, rather immature.

"The song I wrote is titled '66 Sweetheart'; and it came to me when I was reading Plato's theory of forms. He believed that what we see in this world is not the ideal, but only a shadow of perfection; perfection exists in another realm we can never reach except through imagination. To me, beautiful--or near perfect--things we experience in life are close to the ideal and can draw us on to a contemplation of the truth. I blush to write this, but your face, which I saw only briefly years ago, was so nearly perfect that the picture of it has haunted me ever since. It must be close to the ideal form of womanly beauty"

Oh, my goodness, thought Mid. This boy is out of his mind, a hopeless romantic. I trust he's not going to ask me to come to Kansas and sing his song. (Mid did not, in fact, have a very good ear, though she had always appreciated music deeply.)

"What I would like, Miss Lacy, is permission to draw a picture of you to use for my song's artistic representation. I would not identify you in any way to other students or the faculty, but simply present you as the '66 Sweetheart.'"

Well, this seemed harmless. He was no doubt fantasizing, having been struck once by a particular woman and then--blending his memory with the faces of movie stars and other truly beautiful women--he had created a composite image, his own inner vision of a goddess.

"Of course," he went on, "if you were willing to send me a small photograph--an extra one, perhaps, that you don't need--I would be profoundly grateful. Since I'm not a great artist, though a competent one, no one would be led by my portrait to you."

Hmm, this was getting a bit less flattering. Was she beautiful or not?

He added. "I realize the request for a photograph is almost certainly going too far, coming from someone who is a virtual stranger. So, be assured that all I really seek in the end is your permission to think of you and hope what I produce does you some justice."

Mid wondered what would happen if she never responded to this inquiry? Would he go ahead without permission? Or find a 'first runner-up' in his Platonic beauty contest? Give up on the whole project? What a bizarre predicament in which to find herself!

"A final word of explanation about the song, especially its title. As you know, Route 66 is a symbol of the open road, new adventure, American dreams. I have my dreams of making significant

266

contributions to human knowledge. Whether I study medicine or pure mathematics or the mysteries of the physical universe or musical composition, beauty draws me on to new worlds. Your face--at least my memory of it--is my inspiration for this journey."

He closed with an apology if his correspondence in any way embarrassed or upset her; and he included a copy of his song. While the music was also written on a separate sheet, she couldn't read it sufficiently well to hear the tune in her head. She hoped, though, the music would improve the song, which, sadly, did not particularly move her.

> *Angel of love,*
>
> *You are my theme.*
>
> *Hover above,*
>
> *You are my dream.*
>
> > [Refrain]
> >
> > *66 Sweetheart, traveler's star,*
> >
> > *I long to be, wherever you are.*
> >
> > *66 Sweetheart, wings of a dove,*
> >
> > *Lift me to see, spirit of love.*
>
> *Journeying high,*
>
> *You are my dream.*
>
> *Above a sigh,*
>
> *You are my theme.*
>
> > [Refrain]

Oh, my. Mid thought. I don't think my face and this song are going to win any boy $100.00.

She did, though, have an extra, small portrait, taken at her graduation tucked away in her dresser drawer, and she wondered if it would ever be in the hands of a man she loved. What would be the harm, she decided? Nothing will ever come of his composition or of my sending him a picture.

Later, she explained it to herself as an impulse, a product of her frustrating experiences at the time, a silly gesture of misdirected rebellion. Every day she felt her relationship with Tony was the most serious romantic interest of her life. Scientist and his song faded from her daily consciousness, especially whenever Tony came to Macopin.

"Have I ever mentioned Oliver Law?" he asked one night after sharing dinner with the family. Once again the cribbage board was between them. Alice was studying the *Book of Common Prayer* at the dining room table, occasionally explaining Episcopal doctrine to Ethel, who was still cleaning up in the kitchen. Mid had warned Tony not to get caught between them.

"Oliver Law? No, is he another trolley car driver?"

"No, he isn't anything right now. He's dead."

"Oh!" Mid saw Alice look their way and felt a pause in Mother's kitchen activities.

"He died in Spain, in the war. I met him once."

"He died in battle?"

"Yes, but he was the bravest man I ever knew." He hesitated, as if studying his hand to decide what card he would play next. "And he was an American Negro."

268

There was no audible gasp, but a very long pause ensued before Mid said, "I wouldn't have thought . . . I mean over there . . . were there many Negroes?"

"I'm not sure. He had opposed Mussolini's invasion of Ethiopia at home, and I think that drew him to the conflict. Maybe others came, too. Law was also an experienced military man, though, and he had helped organize workers out West. He was a natural born leader."

Mid raised her eyebrows. She knew her mother, endorsing Curtis' beliefs, would not be sympathetic to labor movements or those who organized them. Workers were always getting in the way of good managers who would improve their lot for them.

"He must have had strong feelings, then, to leave this country and . . . " (She realized this country might not seem so wonderful to a Negro) " . . . and those he cared about."

"I think he wanted to take action, and back in this country there were . . . obstacles. You know I've come to realize that not everyone gets a fair shake in life. The hands who work trolley cars, for instance."

Mid thought women didn't always get a fair shake, either. Right now she was being courted, in a sense, by a dreamy romantic out in Kansas and flirted with by a married man at St. Joseph's. What she might want most of all was the chance to embrace a mission that would raise up the unfortunate and earn recognition from others. She couldn't say exactly who or what was to blame, but she felt it was time for her to make a commitment.

Chapter 38: Revelations

A letter from Diana cleared the field of potential aspirants to matrimony with Mid.

"Dearest Mid," Diana wrote. "I know you've wondered about the man I have mentioned who means so much to me. Well, you saw him recently-- he is Bart Stuart."

Mid had to sit down. She'd pulled the letter from the mail, set on the little table by the front door, and was walking toward the kitchen. It was one of her days to cook, and she needed to put her pot roast on the stove. Alice was at her school and Ethel in her room upstairs, probably reading the Bible. Mother had recently finished the Old Testament and was determined to finish the Gospels before Christmas.

"In my travels around the state last year," Diana explained, "I saw Bart perform a number of times. I often organize groups in small towns to come into slightly larger communities for entertainment. Everyone works so hard out here--either in the mines or on farms--that they need recreation. And music is so uplifting."

Mid wondered if anyone in the future would hear the vocalist of a Big Band sing the words, "*Angel of love, / You are my theme, / Hover above, / You are my dream.*" Well, at least one good friend of Mid's had been serenaded by a man who loved her.

"With my study of physiology and my own experience in exercise, I felt sorry at first for Bart.

Most of the time, he would stand to sing, but he had to have help to go very far. At a performance in Elkins, at the school auditorium, his attendant had been called away, and I saw him looking around, so I just stepped up and offered a hand. He was so grateful and so kind in return."

This was like Diana: not only did she have a job helping people, but she noticed other situations where she could take action. Because Diana's brothers were at home, taking care of their parents, she had a certain amount of freedom. Mid believed she was tied down by family duties.

"Anyway, we began to write regularly. And he would send me the band's travel plans, so I could sometimes schedule my work to be where they were. Of course, as you know, he's also from a wealthy family, so he can also go wherever he wants when he's not working. He came to our farm a few weeks ago and requested my parents' permission to ask me to marry him. It's something I never thought would happen--me, to be the wife of a radio star, a man who has such enormous talent. His manager says he might become one of the best in the land."

Mid thought back to Bart's telling her they had "mutual friends." She'd assumed he was referring to Roger and Martha Hartman, who had connections in New York City and might have known Bart's father. They were all from the same social class.

"Now, Mid, you're the first person I'm writing about my engagement; you're still my best friend. There won't be a formal announcement for some months, as a lot of arrangements--which involve lawyers and business matters I don't understand--must be taken care of ahead of time. However, I can tell you I no longer feel sorry for Bart. He's so strong in his commitment to sing, and he never wants sympathy. He's grateful to be alive and to do what he loves to do."

Mid was embarrassed, not just because she also had felt sorry for Bart, but because she'd felt sorry for herself as well. Was she truly restricted as much as she believed?

She returned to Diana's letter. "I'm also writing you for another reason, not just to share my good fortune. In getting to know Bart and the Stuarts, I have concluded that you need to hear something about that family--or at least about Sydney."

While Mid had told Glenna about her "summer romance"--well, she'd given a fictional account of being kissed by Sydney--she'd never discussed him with anyone else at Archer. So, she wasn't sure why Diana would feel Sydney's activities were relevant to her. The trip to the Hippodrome had occurred before she and Diana became fast friends.

"Bart told me about how one of the Stuart vacation homes is close to your family camp in upstate New Jersey. He said you'd all met there once and that Sydney stayed in touch with you afterwards. Sydney didn't tell Bart this, but apparently Bart thinks it's prudent to know about his brother's escapades."

"Escapades"? Mid hardly thought of herself as part of anyone's escapade, especially Sydney Stuart's. Of course, she knew he traveled around the world, and she'd suspected, only half seriously, that he had a "girl in every port." Perhaps that was true after all.

"Bart and Sid have different views, I'm afraid. Perhaps because of his condition, Bart takes other people seriously. He doesn't want them to come to harm. But Sydney is, well, a bit of a playboy. He likes to flirt with the girls wherever he goes. That's not a terrible way to be, but Bart thinks there are times when others have been hurt by his brother. He's never told me any details, saying I don't need to know them. And I'm quite sure they cause him pain."

Mid wondered if Diana thought she had let Sydney go too far. She would have to write back that nothing had happened between them. It was true that there had been times when she regretted Sydney had not seemed more interested; but to Diana it might appear that she had nobly resisted temptation.

"There is one woman--a married woman, unfortunately--who is Sydney's one constant 'friend.' You may even have met her--Samantha Hart is her stage name. She's an actress who lives in New York, but has a husband in New Jersey. If Sydney is ever to settle down, she would have to divorce her husband."

Mid thought about the blond woman she'd seen Sydney escorting into a taxi outside the radio studio. That woman had reminded her of the woman he'd made a point of speaking to at *Lost Horizons*. Could either or both have been Samantha Hart/Mary Hartman? This was a lot for Mid to take in!

273

It was not all she learned that day, however, as Diana continued. "There's one last reason I'm telling you all this, Marian. Bart tells me the Stuarts are a shrewd business family. His father and brother especially use all their charm and worldliness to make people think they are their friends; but sometimes they have other reasons for appearing to take an interest in people."

Mid was sure she would not be counted in this group, as she had no resources an investor might want to attract.

"At one time, the Stuarts thought your father's insurance business might be useful in protecting their properties. They have a number of estates which produce goods that need to be shipped by water. There's a cotton plantation in Missouri, south of St. Louis along the Mississippi river somewhere. And an iron mine not far off Route 66 where there aren't enough freight train lines. So they wanted to use rivers--the Meramec, the St. Francis--for shipping."

Mid recalled the trip she'd taken with Father to St. Louis. Had he been preparing to cooperate with the Stuarts? Could this have been the reason Sydney called on her that fall in Baltimore? Had the accident at Greenwood Lake, when Bill was rescued after turning over his canoe, been the beginning of some sort of improper business scheme?

"Your father was not interested in the proposal Sydney presented to him, according to Bart. But the family apparently thought he would change his mind eventually, so they kept in contact. While Bart isn't sure of all the details, he suspects those Missouri operations aren't very kind to workers. Here in West Virginia we know how mining companies can exploit uneducated and poor workers. And Negroes make up the main labor force in growing cotton. They don't dare raise trouble in that part of the country."

So, Mid had been used to keep the lines of communication open between the two families. She couldn't figure what scheme required an insurance agency's assistance, but maybe there were just associations Father had made over the years they needed. At any rate, she was glad to learn that no improper connections had resulted.

It did make her sad, of course. She was angry not to have been taken seriously, and angry that she'd been naïve about such a possibility. Here she was, graduate of a fine school for women; but because of her status as a woman she'd not had sufficient experience in other spheres to recognize who could be trusted.

She appreciated having known other people, like Tony Giordano, a long time, long enough to have found their loyalty and honesty sound. So, when he made his provisional proposal of marriage at Thanksgiving, she accepted. His honest expression of affection made Roger Hartman's offer of his hand, which came the following week, almost comical.

Chapter 39: Hand of Fate

As if enough weren't already happening in Mid's life, she, Mother, and Alice heard the news over the radio that Pearl Harbor had been attacked. America was at war, and Mid's fiancé enlisted in the Army immediately.

Before now, the primary worry about their union had been religion. Could Mid really convert to a faith her family did not share? She had known of mixed couples, but in all those cases the children were raised Catholic. Would this be acceptable to her or, also important, to Mother? At this point Mid had agreed only to receive initial training in the church.

Tony admitted he was perhaps more a lapsed Catholic than a devout believer, but he would have a hard time ignoring family pressure in such a matter. Agreeing to a long engagement, however, they both believed a solution would be found.

But now her father's reasons for linking her destiny to a soldier also became more significant. With his previous experience on the battlefield, Tony would surely be sent to the front. He could very well be injured or killed. Was she ready for such a trial? She thought about the loss of a lover her uncle had endured, known to her only after he was gone.

A month before her death, Nana had asked to speak to Mid about her son. She had appreciated her grandchild's championing of Henry when he was first found and thought she deserved to understand why he had lived his life so much alone, even after

276

the suspicion of theft was gone. There was another reason beyond the one Mid had known.

Henry Woodruff (become Brickman) had fallen in love with a fragile young woman when they were both teenagers in the countryside beyond Brooklyn. He hadn't yet finished high school, and Ophelia's poor health kept her at home for much of her adolescence. Tuberculosis ran in the family, but they never told Henry. Her stern father simply forbade any talk of courtship and, after a time, refused to let Henry onto his property.

A stubborn young man, Henry floated a canoe down the creek that bordered their land one fall night, and she slipped away with him, carrying a small bag packed with clothes, her few valuables, and a copy of the Bible. She did not drown when the boat turned over, but the resulting chill she caught brought on the fatal attack.

Henry blamed himself for rashness, but also his parents for keeping the truth from him. They'd been taken into confidence by the other family on the condition that they not reveal the nature of Ophelia's sickness. She had a younger sister who seemed to be much more healthy, and they didn't want to restrict the sister's chances for future happiness.

Henry left home to be on his own, eventually securing a position at Starr's Railroad Shipping. But the theft of company funds and the belief that he was suspected led to a second, longer period of depression. If Mid lost Tony, would she have the stoic strength of Henry?

Perhaps because she wasn't sure, she accepted Tony's insistence that his proposal be provisional. "We have to wait until this war is over to marry," he explained. "We can be engaged, but you're free to break the engagement if . . . if I return an invalid."

Mid couldn't help being a bit offended, but for a different reason. "And you can break the engagement if I return injured or . . . compromised in any manner."

"You mean, you'll join in the war effort?"

"If you find it a matter of duty to help your country, shouldn't I feel the same obligation? I have, after all, been preparing to work in a medical capacity wherever the need exists. I may not be able to carry a gun, but I can take up arms, in a sense, to help save others. I'm ready. . . to stand up and be counted in Wayne or in Baltimore or wherever I can." She almost said she was ready to be on the side of the window in the WWI recruiting poster that included marching soldiers, not on the side featuring well-dressed civilians.

Listening to the radio over the next week, she realized much of the nation was ready to march also. She heard that recruiting stations were jammed and many remained open 24 hours a day, seven days a week,. The papers ran stories about how the government was strongly encouraging women to support men who wanted to join, and even to consider volunteering themselves.

Of course, some of her countrymen were reluctant to leave their civilian lives or to embrace a war they viewed as unnecessary, even after American lives

278

had been lost. Roger Hartman (and, Mid speculated, Sydney Stuart) believed they were most useful at home.

"We need better hospitals and more doctors in this effort," Roger told Mid. He'd dropped by her lab to say she would probably be called on more often, as some of the regular workers were already enlisting. "I'm sure I'll be asked to take on new responsibilities myself, both in managing the staff and in developing new treatment programs."

"I'm ready for a larger role as well," Mid responded. "The work I did at Archer might be carried over here, when women begin preparing for different kinds of work. As men become soldiers, the tasks they leave behind must still be performed."

She was also thinking, as she'd told Tony, that she might eventually use the national crisis to pursue her ambition in another place entirely. If Bill continued to be stationed nearby, that would mean more support for Mother at home. Mid didn't think Father James would enlist, so Alice could also remain in the area. Perhaps the moment she'd dreamed about for so many years--the call coming to her from a distant part of the world--was actually approaching.

"There's a greater role you might take on for me, Marian," said Roger, sliding the stool he perched on closer to hers. "My wife and I . . . we're officially estranged now. She's found . . . or I've learned that . . . she has feelings for another man."

Mid leaned back to create more space between them. It occurred to her that he had waited until she was alone to pay this visit. She'd never mentioned

Tony to him or his sister, admitting to herself that Roger's flirtation, although not to be taken seriously, was flattering.

"I'm sorry to hear that, Dr. Hartman. It must be very hard on you."

"Yes, another man, I find, has been her companion for some years. He travels with her when she appears in other cities. Apparently, he's quite wealthy, has estates at home and abroad; he can give her whatever she wants."

"That's terrible. Has he no shame?" She wondered if Samantha Hart had no shame?

He shrugged, looking off into space. "He's the kind of man who enjoys privilege, who has power and connections and prestige inherited from his family."

"I will understand, then, if you're preoccupied now and then. Personal problems can make it difficult to engage your work fully." She realized, with some amusement, that she was drawing on her experience as a counselor in the Fit Female Program to frame her remarks.

He went on, though, as if he'd not heard what she said. "It's true that Mary and I have grown apart in recent years. I didn't realize how much so until . . . until I met you, Marian. Surely, you've realized that . . . I've come to feel a certain . . . desire to be closer to you. Once the separation becomes official, I'd like to . . . call on you, if I may, in a less professional capacity."

He wasn't very professional right now, Mid thought. He's also assuming that she, like any single woman her age, must be looking for a man . . . even a married man.

"Oh, I don't believe that would be appropriate, right now. After all, I work for you here, and . . . " She was having trouble finding the right words. "What are you doing?"

He had stepped off the stool and pushed it to one side with his foot. Then, taking her hand, he lowered himself on one knee before her. She was still sitting on her stool, one leg crossed over the other to create a barrier between them.

"Marian, over the months you've worked here, I believe I've gotten to know you. And, of course, I can't officially ask you to marry me yet, but I have found your beauty to be . . . irresistible. You are a princess, Miss Lacy, an angel. I want you to think of yourself as *my* princess, *my* gift from heaven. Come down from your throne and be with me in an earthly paradise!"

He had gotten flushed as he continued, and his eyes had an odd, hungry look. It was if he saw an image of someone floating in the area where Mid was and wanted to snatch it up, or as if he had, as the saying went, undressed her with his eyes and was feasting on what he saw.

That's when she kicked him.

Well, not exactly. But, releasing his hand, she put her foot on his shoulder and pushed him sufficiently hard that he lost his balance and toppled sideways to the floor. She would have liked to slap him, but

281

decided it would be best to leave him where he was. She walked out of the lab and out of the hospital.

Citing the national crisis and her desire to serve, she resigned from St. Joseph's the next day and began a search that would, in the coming years, take her many miles from New Jersey.

Chapter 40: Moon Woman

Tony's previous experience and the nation's great need took him away from Mid swiftly. His first overseas assignment (in Africa) came early the next year.

Meanwhile, a doctor she had worked with at St. Joseph's begged her to help in the expansion of a veterans' clinic in Newark, anticipating an increase of convalescing soldiers. While it wasn't the kind of service she had contemplated before war broke out, it satisfied her need to be involved immediately. Her responsibilities expanded quickly, and she began to think of this job as the training she needed for a major overseas position in the near future.

Watching the massive mobilization of America, hearing of more losses in the Pacific, and facing an increase of desperate cases in her ward, Marian ignored her own needs. There were moments when she felt like a character in one of Mother's bleak poems:

> *He held his thin cold coat*
> *Tight against the driven rain.*
> *He walked wedging his body thru the wind.*
> *So he struggled with living;*
> *But you knew*
> *His very bones were streaming rain.*
> *Her coat was thin; wind and rain kept coming.*

Many of her neighbors, friends, and co-workers were answering the call of country and preparing for a complete change in their lives. But both Ax's and John's jobs were deemed essential to the war effort, so they continued where they were. And Bill's engineering skills kept him at Fort Dix.

There would be demand for men like Bill Lacy overseas as American forces came fully into action in the spreading conflict. He had the ability to counsel others under stress, improving morale in his outfit and at a little chapel near the base he attended. But his commanders believed such a man could serve most effectively at home for now.

Mother, finally adjusting to widowhood, and Alice, excited at James' formal (accepted) proposal of marriage, regularly offered the wisdom of their religions to Mid, the single Lacy directly connected to a soldier in the field. One referred her to passages in the Bible; the other cited the strength of saints throughout church history.

Yet, over time, they seemed to realize that Mid had her own way of dealing with separation and began to focus more on their own affairs. James had failed his physical (eyesight), so would not be leaving Rutherford. Ethel committed herself to the building of that new church in the community of Macopin, a project that would dominate the rest of her life. The few new poems she wrote from this time on explored the nature of faith and moved away from the modern, experimental style she had pursued earlier.

After the initial period of numbness that lasted into the summer, Marian resolved finally to make the world's upheaval the occasion of her own personal liberation. Whatever Tony's fate, a decision would come from a recognition about her place in the family and in history.

For so many years, she had believed that, when any important selection was to be made, she would be overlooked. While she knew she was loved and respected by her family, she remained the person who would take care of everyone else and thus need little herself. Her calm, steady presence absorbed and controlled the stronger desires of others, almost erasing her from the scene. She was not chosen by the men she desired, who paid more attention to other women--her own sisters, for instance, though she could hardly resent Ella and Alice's good fortune. The eyes of the more privileged Bridges, Hartmans, and Stuarts swept past her as insignificant, unless she might turn out to be useful to them.

She felt that her childhood, college years, and early employment had been staged in a separate realm, insulated from such things as the race of scientific advances, the battle between labor and capital, engines of world conflict. Unlike her friend Diana, she had never had to fight for survival, recover from disaster, build up from nothing. She was protected by a cocoon of social stability and her own innate ability to maintain order.

Lately, though, she had begun to wonder if Tony had not always known her invisible inner self, a woman who needed to be caught up in a cause. Until the last year she had assumed that, like other men, he was creating his version of her based on his own needs. Now she was not so sure; and it made her love him.

Her appreciation strengthened in his absence. What had begun in familiarity and a shared past became more passionate through the letters they exchanged, his often delayed by weeks and even months in transit from more remote (and dangerous) battlefields. This was a man, she found, with whom she believed she could build a family.

In other spheres, however, she was still haunted by the image of her created by Dr. Paterson's poem. The angel floating above earthly problems caught the attention of others, while the living, breathing, struggling Marian was invisible. In another of Mother's poems she found a resemblance between herself and an alien figure in an earthly landscape.

O

moon

woman

I found you

in a garden

your hair blown unbound

earth love entangled you

Mid wanted to be like this unearthly woman-- distinctive but enmeshed in material ties.

She worried that Mother had been missed in her family's view as much as she had: the wife, mother, housekeeper had not been seen as a profound thinker, a published poet who communicated with important writers and journal editors. Mid marveled that a moon woman and a man of bones lived in her mother's imagination--at least, they had at one time. It made her realize that someone so close and apparently so known had a rich, complex, inner life out of sight of her own children--and perhaps unknown to her husband.

Mid considered her other secret identity--66 Sweetheart. The Kansan had sent her a short letter to say he did not win the college song contest that would have helped him in his education; but he was, he wrote, "profoundly grateful" for the photograph she'd sent him. "I keep it with me as a sign of kindness from a distant stranger and as an inspiration to always pursue my dreams."

He did not say what his aspirations were, but the language of his letter contained a curious blend of philosophy and science, celebrating the mysteries of the physical universe as well as the seductive allure of abstract ideas. "Inside the atom lies the ideal; beyond the solar system our light carries the truth." An interesting person at least, Mid concluded.

That she couldn't classify a boy who wrote songs, painted pictures, and planned to be another Einstein made her want to embrace her own identity in her own time: trained medical technologist; fiancée of a soldier away at war; daughter of a widowed mother; sibling of successful, loving brothers and sisters. Her Mother's little poem about the woman in the garden concluded:

287

O strong moon woman
you were the beauty of living
as the wind
  blows

Mid knew she herself was no heavenly creature (Platonic sweetheart or angel rising); she still possessed "the beauty of living." And she knew that "the wind" of history was blowing her forward.

Finally, she accepted the truth about her invisibility: there had been no such thing. She had lived in the midst of powerful currents that shaped her destiny along with everyone else's. Her strong father was struck down by illness, a reminder of human frailty; her youthful professional hopes were blocked (unintentionally) by family obligations and (more conscious) social limitations; the man she had come to believe she should marry was taken away by the spread of evil and his own commitment to combat it. She had never been out of history; she had been in the midst of it all along.

Accepting the fact that her life had not been exempted from the broader patterns of human existence, she set about surveying the landscape before her to determine the new future.

The End

Epilogue: This Far

"This is what I would tell your granddaughter." I held my right hand up horizontally in front of my face. Then I brought my forefinger over to a point just above the top of my thumb, making a shape that might, in shadow puppetry, create a bird's head and beak. It was my sign for things being so close they're almost touching. "You're this far."

"That's how close she is to heaven?" Curtis asked. "I thought you told five-year-olds that angels are way up there in the sky." He waved a hand vaguely over his head.

"I'm thinking of what my father used to say, a universal answer to a child's question."

I pictured Father smiling, a sly look on his face while he made this gesture, whenever we asked him how close we were to Greenwood Lake or if we had much more to walk before we reached the ice cream shop at which we would be treated to sundaes.

His grandson, my younger son, didn't understand me. "I had enough trouble," he said, "explaining how putting a dead parakeet in a shoebox in the ground was sending him to God. Abigail kept looking down at the little grave in the garden and then back up at me. I don't see how telling her heaven was 'this far' away would help."

I'd been in Abigail's shoes myself, of course, though it was a kitten I mourned ninety years ago. And Curtis experienced the same disbelief when he was seven and lost Major. We're all the same in having to go through childhood tragedies.

He went on. "How did a grandparent get the job of making death seem an easy journey to heaven, anyway?"

I chuckled. He was being at least partially facetious, having had these conversations with his own children decades earlier. He was primarily entertaining me, providing the great-grandmother with something to talk about and share with others at the retirement complex.

"You're giving the right answers. It's just that she has to live a few more years before they make sense to her. Haven't I told you about that time when I had to find the right carbon paper for my boss? It was when I was attending a meeting in Washington, D.C."

"Carbon paper? To make copies." Curtis hesitated, as he often will when he is thinking more about what needs to be said than about the truth. He's an English professor, so he believes you should weigh what you might say against the expectations of your audience. At times, it's infuriating, but I know he is convinced the truth can be delivered in indirect ways.

"If you did, I fear I've forgotten about it. Was this when you were working at St. Joseph's."

"No it was after that. It was . . . it was not long before I left Rutherford and Macopin."

What I really meant was that it was during the time I was grieving for Tony. He was killed on the ground with the 1st Armored Division near Tunisia late in the first year of the war. I almost never talk about that difficult time. In fact, I've generally kept quiet even about the years after I finished at Archer and before I went west on my own. Curtis's father liked to feel I had no romantic interests before him, and--always the considerate wife!--I indulged him by skipping over my relationships with men back east in recounting my history.

I went on to Curtis. "I was 'this far' from carbon paper, but didn't know it. The staff at the convalescent clinic for soldiers were always having to travel to Washington and convince the government we needed more money, more supplies, more support."

"You'd think that would have been obvious."

"Well, so many organizations were struggling with limited resources in those months. You know there was rationing of gasoline and certain foods, many things. So, we got there, had to produce more statements (in triplicate!), and found that the box of carbon paper we'd bought from the office was faulty. Of course, carbon paper was available at any stationary store, so I volunteered to step out and purchase some."

"They wasn't any at the agency where you were?"

I laughed. "You academics are so innocent about the workings of the real world. Of course, they were available, but only with the correct requisition order, approval from the necessary offices, and after the appropriate time for processing."

"Ah, so the carbon paper was . . . this far away." He copied the bird's beak gesture with his forefinger and thumb. "But you couldn't touch it."

"That's right. And men back then felt getting supplies was beneath them, even though it was a miserable day in the nation's capital, especially for April--barely above freezing, a strong wind blowing rain, dark skies all around.""

I launched into the story with enthusiasm, but also with a bit of sadness. Talking to Curtis about that period brought back painful memories. I have gotten so good at repressing the experience of losing Tony that, when it popped to the surface from so deep in my consciousness today, I was suddenly teary. So much for my advice about those we love always being with us!

Tony, by the way, received numerous posthumous commendations for valor; but, even following newspaper accounts and recalling Dr. Royal's stories of events from the Great War, I had great difficulty connecting the descriptions of actions I read with a world I knew from experience. For me, the distant and foreign had shattered the familiar and close at hand. I found myself seeking any means to put my world back together--or a way to create an entirely new one. That I am now more able to match what happened to its telling is a mixed blessing.

"I was sure," I told Curtis, "that I'd seen a stationery shop in the block we'd had to walk past from the bus stop. So I trudged over there, my umbrella in danger of being inverted at any minute by the wind, and my feet getting wet in all the puddles. When I stopped under an awning and scanned the row of shops across the street, there was no stationery shop. Not even a drug store or department store."

Curtis understood immediately. "It's like when you search the storage closet--in your mind's eye, of course--and are sure you see the old Candy Land game up on the top shelf; but when you go to look, it's not there."

"That's exactly the way it was that day. I had a mental picture of a stationery shop--two big windows on the sides of an entrance with displays of letters, envelopes, pens--everything that would suggest carbon paper inside. I was confident it had been on this street."

"And you didn't want to return without the carbons. Where else could you look?"

"There wasn't anywhere close, at least as far as I knew." I remembered my unhappiness at that moment; it was way out of proportion. "I was trying hard to please everyone in those days!"

"Well, now it's our job to please you." He smiled and patted my arm. He means it, too.

"I should think so!" I told him. "At any rate, there I stood, getting colder and damper by the minute, the rain rolling off the awning in front of me in sheets. I had no idea where to go." I paused for dramatic effect, smiling at the memory of seventy years ago.

"And then I noticed . . . or I felt . . . I hadn't even turned my head at first . . . but somehow I knew that there was this big sign over my right shoulder. Bold black letters in a large white block. So I turned around and read the words: 'Ben Nix's Letters.'"

"That was a stationery store?"

"There were Nix shops in major cities all across the country. You see, I was standing right in front of the place I had been looking for! It was . . . " I chuckled and held up my hand again, the index finger reaching across to the thumb. " . . . this far!"

"That's fantastic. And I trust you got all sorts of praise when you returned."

"Of course not. They had no idea how hard it had been or how lucky I was. They just assumed it was an easy task, and they knew me as a person who could get things done."

I was rewarded, however, not by a boss's compliment but by the gaining of wisdom. It's not easy to believe when you're young, but the older I get the more I am convinced we're only 'this far' from everyone we've ever loved, from all we've done in life, from what makes us human.

Oh, sure, there is physical space that separates bodies, and we must travel over distances to hold each other. But our spirits are connected: mine and Tony's, mine and Curtis's father, all my brothers and sisters--gone from this world, of course, but they are with me in this one still.

"Mom, you're just full of stories!"

"That's why we're talking. Before I turn into the angelic version of me in heaven (I'm just the carbon copy in this lower world), I want to deliver all my secrets to you. When you come next weekend, I'm going to start in on the next tale you need to hear and share."

"I can't wait!"

He is a good boy, isn't he!

Ω

Route 66 books by Michael Lund

Growing Up on Route 66 — Michael Lund (2000) ISBN 1-888725-31-1 Novel evoking fond memories of what it was like to grow up alongside "America's Highway" in 20th Century Missouri. (Trade paperback) 5x8 260 pp

Route 66 Kids — Michael Lund (2002) ISBN 1-888725-70-2 Sequel to *Growing Up on Route 66*, continuing memories of what it was like to grow up alongside "America's Highway" in 20th Century Missouri. (Trade paperback) 5x8 270 pp,

A Left-hander on Route 66--Michael Lund (2003) ISBN 1-888725-88-5. Twenty years after the fact, left-hander Hugh No one appeals a wrongful conviction that detoured him from "America's Main Street" and put him in jail. But revealing the details of the past and effecting a resolution of his case mean a dramatic rearrangement of his world, including troubled relationships with three women: Linda Roy, Patty Simpson, and Karen Murphy. (Trade paperback) 5x8 270 pp

Route 66 Spring-- Michael Lund (2004) ISBN: 1-888725-98-2. The lives of four young Missourians are changed when a bottle comes to the surface of one of the state's many natural springs. Inside is a letter written by a girl a dozen years after the end of the Civil War. Lucy Rivers Johns ' epistle contains a sad story of family failure and a powerful plea for help. This message from the last century crystallizes the individual frustrations of Janet Masters, Freddy Sills, Louis Clark, and Roberta Green, another group of Route 66 kids. Their response to the past charts a bold path into the future, a path inspired by the Mother Road itself. (Trade paperback) 5x8 270 pp.

Miss Route 66--Michael Lund (2004) ISBN 1-888725-96-6. In the fourth novel of Michael Lund's Route 66 Novel

Series, Susan Bell tells the story of her candidacy in Fairfield, Missouri's annual beauty contest. Now married and with teenage children in St. Louis, she recounts her youthful adventure in this small town along "America's Highway." At the same time, she plans a return to Fairfield in order to right injustices she feels were done to some young contestants in the Miss Route 66 Pageant. (Trade paperback) 5 X8, 260 pp, **Audio book** on 5 CD's ISBN 1-888725-12-5

Route 66 to Vietnam Michael Lund (2004) ISBN 1-59630-000-0 This novel takes characters from earlier works in the Route 66 Novel Series farther west than Los Angeles, official destination of the famous highway, Route 66. Mark Landon and Billy Rhodes find the values they grew up on challenged by America's role in Southeast Asia. But elements of their upbringing represented by the Mother Road also sustain them in ways they could never have anticipated. . (Trade paperback) 5 X8, 270 pp,.

Audio Book on CD—Route 66 to Vietnam ISBN: 1-59630-011-6 Michael Lund's fictional commentary from the viewpoint of a draftee. by Michael Lund unabridged 6 CD's --9 hours running time

Route 66 Chapel Michael Lund (2006) ISBN 1-59630-012-4 Route 66 Chapel, Michael Lund (2006) (Trade paperback) 5 X8, 260 pp. When the forces of progress threaten the foundation of small-town life—a small church—five senior citizens, a mysterious newcomer, and one young couple band together in an unlikely campaign to save it. The embattled meeting point of old and new is Route 66 Chapel, a building curiously linked to America's "Mother Road."

Route 66 Choir-- A Comedy (2010) Michael Lund ISBN 9781596300583 284 pp 5" x 8" In Route 66 Choir Stanley Measure takes early retirement just before September 11, 2001, and his impulsive decisions participate in an

297

unraveling of confidence in the American way of life. His wife Felicia finds that everything she holds dear is in danger of coming apart: her marriage, her church, her business, and even her country. Who or what can orchestrate the recovery of harmony necessary to sustain the spirit of the Mother Road?

Route 66 Sweetheart (2011) ISBN 9781596300705   304pp 5"x8". This first of a novel series chronicles an American family during times of peace and war from 1915 to 2015. The first book, *Route 66 Sweetheart*, is set mostly in and around Rutherford, New Jersey, during the 1930s, where a young woman who traces her ancestry back to the early New World settlement of Nantucket comes to maturity during the Depression In the shadows of an emerging World War II.

Educators' Discount Policy

To encourage use of our books for education, educators can purchase three or more books (mixed titles) on our standard discount schedule for resellers. See **sciencehumanitiespress.com** for more detail or call Science & Humanities Press, PO Box 7151, Chesterfield MO 63006-7151   phone 1-636-394-4950